BLOODSHED AT THE OWL BLIND DEC30

BELL BECK

CHAPTER 1

Logs popped and crackled in the fireplace, sending tiny sparks scattering across the lodge's century-old stone hearth. Beyond the windows, the morning sun danced on a fresh blanket of snow, while inside, the comforting scents of freshly brewed coffee and baking pastries floated through the great room.

It was another perfect winter morning in the Adirondacks.

Well, almost perfect.

A few minutes ago the kid from Cabin 4 had dropped an entire jar of jelly on the hardwood floor, sending strawberry globs and glass shards everywhere. While I was on my hands and knees cleaning up that mess, two older ladies informed me that the decaf coffee was, in fact, caffeinated. Thanks to me, they wouldn't sleep for the next two days.

And if one more person asked me about gluten-free scones, I was going to lose it.

Last summer, I would have traded a pinky toe for a packed lodge. Now, it was the middle of January, and doubts were creeping in as we scrambled to accommodate a surge of nature enthusiasts.

My brilliant idea to add a breakfast bar? Not so brilliant after all. Way to go, Honey Palmer.

The chaos started when a wave of snowy owls swooped into our little town of Beechtree shortly after New Year's. Though the Adirondacks usually saw a few snowy owls during the winter months, this was a full-on, feathered invasion. Our birding festival last July had put Loon Lodge on the map, and now it seemed like every bird lover and and their brother needed a place to stay.

The lodge wasn't alone. Every small business in Beechtree was dealing with similar challenges. While we all prepared for the summer tourist season by adding staff, we operated with skeleton crews during the winter months. January was supposed to be our slowest time of the year.

A familiar voice snapped me back to reality. "Remind me, how long are these snowy owls expected to stay?"

Evie Hicks-Turner held a third ownership stake in Loon Lodge. More importantly, she was my best friend. Following the sale of her marketing firm, she tagged along for a leisurely summer retreat to the mountains and quickly fell in love with my family's dilapidated hospitality venture. It wasn't long before we both decided to relocate here, and Evie invested some of her savings in the business to help fund much-needed renovations.

I stood up, folding the last of the jelly jar bits into a kitchen towel. "That depends on the owls," I replied. "They could stick around for a few more days or a few more months. They go where the grub is."

Evie gestured toward a new wave of guests converging on the breakfast bar. "They're not the only ones following the food supply," she whispered.

I tossed the towel into a trash bin and picked up a serving

tray to help clear the tables. "Well, if there's one thing we can count on," I said, gathering up napkins and leftover bits of English muffins, "it's that this hungry flock isn't going anywhere."

Right on cue, a middle-aged guy with a beer belly and salt-and-pepper goatee ambled over to us. Decked out in full camo, he told us that the breakfast bar was out of cream cheese. "You're running low on bagels too," he added before wandering back to his table.

Evie shook her head, bewildered. "I've got this. Might as well get another pot of coffee brewing while I'm at it," she said and headed to the kitchen, balancing a tray of dirty dishes on her arm.

After tidying the chairs around the table, I took a look around the great room. The rest of the lodge was still a work in progress, but this room was among the first we had renovated, and its makeover was nothing short of spectacular.

Despite its grand scale, the room oozed coziness. Overhead, wooden beams criss-crossed the high ceiling, while a pair of rustic chandeliers hung down, casting a warm, welcoming light throughout the space.

On the second floor, guest rooms lined the hallway. Balcony railings offered an ideal vantage point for soaking in the ambiance of the great room below and provided stunning views of Beechtree Lake through the large picture windows along the far wall.

The furnishings were no less impressive. Cafe tables and chairs, ingeniously crafted from twisted branches and logs, were interspersed among plush sofas and armchairs, inviting guests to relax with a good book and a hot drink.

The crown jewel was a magnificent two-story fireplace, constructed from fieldstones culled from the property more than a hundred years ago. Its mantle proudly displayed an assortment of keepsakes, each one telling a story from the lodge's long history.

Facing the fireplace, on the room's opposite side, we had set up a temporary exhibit dedicated to the snowy owls. When owl watchers started pouring into town, we'd run ourselves ragged trying to field their questions while also handling the lodge's day-to-day operations. We needed help, and we needed it fast.

By sheer luck, Twilla Jankowsky, a college friend of my daughter Maddie, happened to be passing through Beechtree when the owls arrived in town. As a young conservationist between jobs, she happily took charge of the info station so we could focus on lodge operations. Her encyclopedic knowledge of owls and other forms of wildlife was amazing.

A little too amazing, actually.

News of her expertise spread quickly, and it wasn't long before Loon Lodge became owl central. For the past few weeks, people had streamed in and out of the lodge all day long to warm up by the fire and swap stories about the latest sightings. Whether they were staying with us or just passing through, the increased traffic was a boon for visibility, and I was thrilled to see people excited about birdwatching, despite the toll it took on us to keep everything running smoothly.

Across the room, I saw Twilla setting up the info station. With brunette hair that cascaded down her shoulders and a smile that lit up the room, she was a hit with guests. It was easy to see why.

As I approached the station, I noticed her chatting with a tall, rugged-looking man dressed in a parka. His broad shoulders, chiseled features, and tousled hair hinted at time spent in the outdoors, and the gleam in Twilla's eyes suggested he was making quite an impression.

"Morning, Twilla. Everything under control?" The hunk

in the parka looked familiar, though I couldn't figure out where I'd seen him before.

"Yep, we're all set here. Just having a chat with our guest, Mason," Twilla responded, motioning toward the hunk.

Mason introduced himself as a photographer, and that's when it hit me – he was Mason Reed, a familiar name in birding circles. Known for his out-of-this-world wildlife photography, one of his recent photos—a shot of the northern lights reflected in the eye of an Arctic wolf—had recently garnered international acclaim.

A flutter of excitement rippled through me as Mason shook my hand. "Nice to meet you, Honey," he said, his voice deep and commanding.

"It's a pleasure to meet you too," I replied, doing my best to maintain my composure. "I'm a huge fan of your work. Your photographs are phenomenal."

Mason broke into a toothy smile. "Thank you so much. I suppose it's pretty obvious why I'm here. I'm hoping to add some snowy owl photographs to my portfolio in the coming days."

"Well, you definitely came to the right place," I said, pointing at the info table and owl exhibit. "We have plenty of resources to help you find them."

"I've already gotten some great advice from Twilla here," he responded, sending a playful wink her way.

"Actually, we're hosting another wildlife photographer at the moment," I said. "Ollie Harlow. Have you heard of him?"

"We've crossed paths," Mason replied, but his tone suggested there was more to the story. As he looked across the room, he added, "Speak of the devil."

Following his gaze, I noticed an older man weaving through the crowd. With white hair and weathered features, he wore a thick puffer jacket and a camera bag hung from his shoulder.

"Reed," he said, rolling up to the info station. "Still pretending to be a wildlife photographer, I see."

"Not sure what you're talking about, Ollie. I'm just here taking epic shots, just like every other world-class wildlife photographer." The corner of Mason's mouth lifted into a smirk. "Though, I'm not sure that's something you'd know much about these days."

"Oh, we're all quite familiar with how you get your 'epic shots,'" Ollie replied, his voice thick with sarcasm.

Twilla extended her hand. "I don't believe we've met yet."

"No, we haven't," Ollie scoffed, then turned to me. "There's nobody at reception, and the bathroom faucet in my cabin won't stop leaking. It's driving me insane. I've been out late taking night shots, and that constant dripping makes it impossible to get any rest."

"I'll make sure someone checks it out later this morning," I assured him.

"Please do," he growled and stomped toward the door. Stopping mid-stride, he spun around to face Twilla. "And you, if you really want to be of help, you'd put a stop to all this right now," he said, motioning at the info station. "The last thing this place needs is more hobbyists in the field, disturbing the wildlife and interfering with the work of professionals."

As he stormed off, Twilla's eyes followed him across the room. If looks could kill, Ollie would have dropped dead somewhere in the vicinity of the beverage station.

Mason placed a gentle hand on Twilla's shoulder. "Ignore him. Ollie's just a bitter old has-been. What you're doing here matters, and it's making a difference."

I slipped away to finish clearing tables, leaving Twilla and Mason to carry on their conversation. Mason seemed like a decent guy, but Ollie? He was a piece of work. I hoped they would keep their distance from each other at the lodge, but I decided to keep an eye on them, just in case.

As I finished clearing the last table, the mom from Cabin 4 came over.

"Sorry about that jelly jar mess," she said with a laugh. "Kids, huh? What are you gonna do?"

I had a few suggestions about what she might do to rein in her little tornado, but I held my tongue and assured her it was no big deal.

"Since I have you here," she went on, "I just have to tell you how much we love the lodge. The scenery is breathtaking, and the breakfast looks absolutely tempting. But we do have some dietary restrictions. Is there any chance you offer a gluten-free version of the scones?"

I stifled a scream.

It was going to be another long day at Loon Lodge.

CHAPTER 2

*A*s the morning rush slowed down to a steady trickle, Evie and I finally found a moment to catch our breath and dive into the myriad other duties that came with running a mountain lodge.

The arrival of the owls had forced us to modify some of our normal routines to accommodate the influx of guests. Right out of the gate, we'd reduced daily housekeeping services to emptying bins and swapping out used towels. While guests had the option to request additional cleaning services, that minor change alone had saved us a ton of time.

We'd also started outsourcing our laundry to a local service, moving away from our ancient in-house washer and dryer. It was an extra expense, but eliminating laundry from our daily to-do list was more than worth it.

Despite those changes, Evie and I still had a full day's work ahead of us. After closing down the breakfast bar and refilling the coffee urns one last time, Evie took over the front desk duties, and I retreated to the office to tackle the overnight reservation requests.

Following a quick lunch break, Evie then handed off

front desk duties to my father, Fuzz, so we could prepare rooms for arriving guests and collect discarded trash and towels from the current ones.

Fuzz had inherited the lodge from his own father years ago and recently brought Evie and me on board as co-owners. Since the onset of the owl invasion, he'd spent mornings snowplowing the parking lot, shoveling walkways, and tackling various odd jobs, like fixing Ollie Harlow's leaky faucet.

With our housekeeping duties done for the day, we returned to the lodge and discovered Fuzz fast asleep at the front desk. His loyal companion—a burly, tan-and-white standard poodle named Charley—slumbered at his feet.

Evie pressed a finger to her lips, then crept over to the desk and surprised Fuzz with a big, wet kiss. His eyes popped open, and he jerked backward, nearly tipping over the desk chair. When he regained his balance, he leaned into it and energetically reciprocated her affection.

Evie and Fuzz's romance had really taken off since last summer, and while I was truly happy for them, their public displays of affection were starting to grate on me.

He eventually broke away, wearing a big smile. "Sorry, kiddo," he apologized, "we get carried away sometimes."

I rolled my eyes, only half-amused. "How about toning it down a bit next time, Fuzz?"

Born Henry Stillman, I gave my father the nickname Fuzz when I was a little girl, on account of his big, bushy beard. The name stuck and from then on, everyone in Beechtree knew him as Fuzz. It would have felt weird for both of us if I called him Dad now.

Roused by the commotion, Charley lifted his head and thumped his tail on the floor, sizing up the situation. When he realized it was just me and Evie, he laid back down and quickly drifted back to sleep.

Just then, the lodge's hefty wooden door groaned open, and a pair of elderly guests, the Carusos, entered the lobby. Evie quickly slid off Fuzz's lap as the husband-and-wife duo brushed the snow from their boots onto the entryway mat.

What Fred and Lois Caruso lacked in birdwatching skills, they made up for in enthusiasm. New to the world of birding, they'd packed up their camper van and embarked on the twelve-hour trek from Cincinnati as soon as they heard about the snowy owls. Since arriving at the lodge a week ago, they'd ventured out before dawn every day, returning in late afternoon.

Just the other day, Evie cracked a joke about how Fred, with his round body and spindly legs, resembled a giant owl. Round eyeglasses perched on the end of his nose completed the look.

Lois appeared more refined, her silver locks coiled into a loose bun. Both Carusos were dressed for cold weather in bulky down jackets, insulated trousers, and sturdy hiking boots.

"Welcome back, Carusos! How was the owl watching today?" Fuzz asked as they approached the front desk.

Before Lois could answer, Fred launched into an animated recap of their day. peppering. He included way too many details, but his excitement seemed genuine, and I found myself smiling along.

Before Lois could get a word in, Fred launched into a lively recap of their day, sprinkling in way more details than necessary. But his enthusiasm was infectious, and I found myself smiling along.

When he finally stopped to take a breath, I jumped at the chance to ask if he or Lois needed anything.

"Now that you mention it, would it be possible to use the kitchen to make a hot toddy before bed?" Fred asked. "Our room doesn't have a microwave, and a toddy is just the thing to warm up after a chilly day outside."

"Fred zonks out the moment he's horizontal, but not me. I wrestle with insomnia till the wee hours," Lois chimed in. "It's soothing to sit by the fire and read, and it would be wonderful to have access to the microwave so I could make some tea too."

The Carusos were staying in an upstairs room, which, unlike the cabins, lacked a kitchenette. I empathized with Lois' sleep struggles. I'd experienced my fair share of sleepless nights a few years back. Just one of the joys of middle age.

"Of course," I replied, "but let's keep it our little secret, okay?" The last thing I wanted was for the kid in Cabin 4 to think the kitchen was open for late-night foraging.

"Thank you, my dear," Fred said, then caught me off guard with a friendly peck on the cheek before the pair disappeared upstairs.

"What do you think? Should we make a new rule that guests have to give us a kiss if they want after-hours kitchen access?" Evie asked, a sparkle in her eye.

I chuckled. "And what happens if they say no?"

"Then, they don't get any hot toddies!" Fuzz grinned.

As the afternoon wound down, Fuzz closed the front desk and took Charley for one last look around the lodge. Meanwhile, Evie and I spent the next half hour setting up for the following morning's breakfast bar.

With breakfast sorted out, it was time to call it a day. And not a moment too soon—I was beat.

On our way out, we stopped in the great room to straighten up the furniture. "Is Sam coming over tonight?" Evie asked. "I haven't seen him around much lately."

When I returned to Beechtree last summer, I was fresh off a divorce and had no intention of jumping back into the dating scene. Yet somehow, I'd found myself in a committed relationship with Sam Abbott, owner of the Beechtree Mercantile. We usually ended our days with dinner at my cabin, but the influx of owl enthusiasts had disrupted our usual routine.

"I doubt it," I answered, stifling a yawn. "He's tied up at the mercantile, and you know how busy we've been here at the lodge. Besides, I'm not sure I have the energy for a date night."

"Same here," Evie agreed. "I could fall asleep right here."

A blast of cold air slammed into us as we stepped outside. Though winter in Beechtree meant frigid temperatures and ungodly amounts of snow, I couldn't imagine living anywhere else.

"Catch you later, Evie," I called out as we parted ways.

"Night, Honey," she said and headed toward the cabin she shared with Fuzz at the south end of the property.

Trudging through the snow to my cabin, I took a mental inventory of my freezer. A frozen pizza sounded perfect, followed by a quick shower, and then straight to bed.

Morning would be here before I knew it.

THE VIBRATION of my phone on the nightstand jolted me awake. Still groggy, I reached for it and mumbled a groggy hello. It was Sam, and he sounded much more awake than I felt.

"Rise and shine, Honey Palmer," he said, his voice like a warm blanket on an icy morning.

"Hey you. What's up?"

"Just checking in on my best girl. I'm starting to miss our dinners."

"I miss them too," I admitted, pushing myself up into a

sitting position. "It's been all hustle and bustle here at the lodge with the owl watchers."

"Why don't you take a little break and stop by the mercantile later? The coffee's terrible, but the company's the best in town."

It was a tempting offer. As much as I enjoyed spending time with Sam, the idea of stepping away from the lodge, even for a little while, felt impossible. We couldn't maintain this pace much longer. Something had to give.

"I'll see what I can do, Sam, but no promises. It's pretty nutso over here."

We said our goodbyes, and I reluctantly emerged from the snug cocoon of my bedcovers. Though my muscles protested, I threw on a fleece and cargo pants, then layered up with a parka and beanie before making my way to the lodge.

By eight-thirty, the great room hummed with activity. Evie and I were busy restocking the breakfast bar for the late risers when the Carusos arrived. Fred seemed more subdued than normal, while Lois looked pale and worn out.

"You're back early," I said. "Everything alright?"

Lois managed a weak smile, then slowly headed toward the stairs. Fred hung back, shedding his coat and scarf with a heavy sigh.

"Lois isn't feeling well this morning," he explained. "She probably just needs some rest. Could you leave the towels outside our door today?"

"You bet, Fred," Evie responded. "Anything else? Maybe some tea for Lois?"

"Thank you, dear, but no." His tone was warm and paternal, though he didn't appear much older than Evie herself. "She just needs some rest. All those late-night reading sessions downstairs are taking their toll."

He followed Lois up the stairs, and as they disappeared

from view, I noticed the info station was vacant. In the midst of the breakfast rush, the info station had completely slipped my mind.

"Evie, have you seen Twilla around today?"

"Nope," Evie said, eyeing the deserted info station. "She's normally here first thing. I bet she'll turn up any minute," she added, before heading back into the kitchen.

A little while later, I was arranging a tray of freshly baked blueberry muffins when Twilla finally appeared, quick-stepping her way across the great room. "Someone wants to see you at the front desk," she said. Then, leaning in closer, she whispered, "It's the police."

The police? That couldn't be good. The last time law enforcement paid a visit to the lodge was back in July, when the mayor of Beechtree was found dead at Warblers' End, a popular birdwatching spot on the property. Though everything got sorted out in the end, that week was an absolute circus.

I set the muffin tray aside, slipped off my flour-coated apron, and made a beeline for the front desk. Along the way, I tried to reassure myself that it was probably nothing, no need to jump to conclusions.

A stern-faced deputy from the Beechtree Police Department was waiting for me in the lobby, impatiently thumbing through a notepad. I mustered a polite smile and introduced myself.

"So, how can I assist you, officer?"

The deputy creased his brow. "I'm here about one of your guests," he said, consulting his notepad. "A fellow named Ollie Harlow. Is he a guest here?"

"Uh, yeah, Ollie's staying with us. What's going on?" I asked.

The deputy closed his notepad with a snap and tucked it away. "Mr. Harlow was found dead this morning."

"Dead?" I exclaimed. "I just saw him yesterday, and he seemed perfectly fine."

"Afraid so. We confirmed his identity with his license, and he had a room key from your lodge on him."

A lump formed in my throat. "What happened?"

"That's what we're trying to figure out," he answered. "The chief will be here shortly, but in the meantime, he's asked me to secure Mr. Harlow's room. Could you take me to it?"

I led the deputy to Ollie's cabin, questions swirling in my head. Hopefully I'd learn more when the chief arrived, but for now, one thing seemed crystal clear...

The circus was back in town.

CHAPTER 3

I left the deputy stationed in his cruiser outside Ollie's cabin and returned to the lodge. After sharing the news about Ollie with Evie and Fuzz, I kept myself busy in the kitchen, making sure I had a clear view of the driveway through the window above the sink.

Before long, a white SUV pulled up, its lights flashing, side panels emblazoned with the words "Beechtree Police" in bold green letters.

From my vantage point, I watched a short, skinny man in a tan uniform emerge from the SUV. Big Ted Dibley. His service jacket displayed an oversized badge, and he wore a standard-issue police trapper hat. After a brief exchange with his deputy, he strode across the parking lot toward the lodge, his black utility belt bouncing against his bony hips.

The breakfast crowd was thinning out, so I grabbed Evie and put Fuzz in charge of the breakfast bar. Given the history between Fuzz and Big Ted during the Warblers' End incident, I thought it was probably best to keep them separated.

Evie and I greeted Big Ted in the lobby, then led him

through a wood-paneled hallway to our office. As he sauntered down the corridor, he took in the photos on the walls, stopping at a picture of the lodge before the cabins were added, when the parking area was just a patch of earth.

"This place has really changed over the years, hasn't it?" he asked, studying the photo.

"It sure has," I said, "and we have more changes in store."

Big Ted snorted his disapproval. Apparently, he wasn't a fan of change.

Once we were in the office, he slowly eased into an armchair. He'd accepted the gig of part-time police chief after retiring, and it seemed the surge of owl watchers in town was starting to wear him down too.

"I'm not sure how much my deputy told you, but early this morning, a couple of those owl people stumbled on your guest, Ollie Harlow, at Hayes Landing. He was frozen solid, stiff as a board," he said, leaning back in his chair. "Any idea what Harlow might have been doing out there?"

"It doesn't take a rocket scientist to figure that out," Evie said. "Ollie was a professional wildlife photographer, and Hayes Landing has been a hotspot for snowy owls for the past two weeks."

"Snowy owls prefer open spaces, especially airports or deserted airfields like Hayes Landing," I explained. "It reminds them of where they come from. You know, Arctic tundras and all."

He nodded slowly, absorbing the information. "So, you're saying he ventured out there in the dead of night to photograph these owls that everyone's buzzing about?"

"I think that's a pretty safe assumption," I said. "Photographers like Ollie live for the perfect wildlife shot. Sometimes, they even take photos at night. A snowy owl irruption like this is rare, and I'm sure he wanted to make the most of it.

Although snowy owls aren't strictly nocturnal, they're often active at night."

Big Ted looked confused. "Eruption? Like a volcano?"

"Not even close. It's a term for an unexpected surge of birds in a place they're not typically seen," Evie elaborated.

"Okay," he pondered, rubbing his chin. "Here's something you might find interesting. When we inspected the body, we found numerous cuts and puncture marks on Harlow's face and neck. It looked like he'd taken a pretty nasty blow to the head too."

He shifted uncomfortably in his seat before continuing. "And one of his eyes was gone. Plucked clean out. Almost like he'd been attacked by a large bird or something."

He glanced over with his bushy eyebrows raised, waiting for a response. Evie and I exchanged a look. The bit about the eyeball was kind of grim, but I could tell we were both thinking the same thing.

"You're not suggesting an owl is behind this, are you?" I asked incredulously.

"I'm just exploring every angle here. But I did see a documentary once about a woman from North Carolina, some Peterson lady. She was attacked and killed by an owl. It happened right in her own backyard!"

I didn't want to completely dismiss him, but the idea of a killer owl was beyond far-fetched.

"I'm familiar with the case you're talking about, and even the experts said it was highly unusual. If I remember correctly, most of the woman's injuries happened when she fell down a flight of stairs."

"Actually," Evie interjected, "her husband was found guilty of her murder. He went to prison and everything."

Big Ted was unconvinced. "Maybe, but I'd like to hear what that owl gal of yours has to say." Hoisting himself from the chair, he said, "Why don't you take me to her, and we'll have a chat."

Fuzz was nowhere to be found as we escorted Big Ted through the great room. Along the way, I noticed several guests staring at us, no doubt wondering why Evie and I were parading a guy bearing an uncanny resemblance to Barney Fife through the lodge.

We found Twilla at the info station, talking with a group of owl watchers. I noticed she had expanded the display with several new additions. Her collection was a treasure trove of owl-related curiosities: feathers, an intact owl skeleton, and several preserved owl pellets—regurgitated masses of undigested bones, fur, feathers, and other parts of prey animals that owls consume.

"Twilla, this is Big Ted, the police chief here in Beechtree," I said.

"Pleasure to meet you!" Twilla gave his hand a hearty shake. "Are you here for information on the owls?"

"In a way, I suppose I am," he answered. "I hear you're something of an expert on these birds."

"I wouldn't say I'm an expert, but I can tell you everything you need to know about our snowy owl irruption," Twilla began. "This year, the Adirondacks are seeing an unusual number of snowies, and it's pretty exciting. And why is that, you ask? Well, it's because . . ."

Twilla dove into a lengthy explanation of the habitats and migration patterns of snowy owls, describing how irruptions are driven by food scarcities in the owls' Arctic breeding grounds. When the lemming population declines, some owls venture south in search of alternative prey, leading them to places with a greater number of rodents, like northern New York.

Big Ted let her go on for a while before cutting her off.

"Okay, okay, but what I really need to know is whether one of these owls could kill a person?"

The question caught Twilla off guard. "Kill someone? You have to understand that snowy owl attacks are extremely rare. Their talons are designed for hunting small prey like lemmings and voles. See for yourself." She reached for a set of talons in the exhibit. When she picked them up, a look of confusion flickered across her face.

Composing herself, she went on, "The only time a snowy owl might show even a little aggression is when they're defending a nest. During irruptions, it's usually the younger owls that migrate south, like we're seeing now. And they don't have any nests to defend."

"But one of these owls could inflict serious injuries on a person, right?" Big Ted persisted. "Maybe even gouge out an eye?"

I cleared my throat. "Twilla's right. It's virtually unheard of for owls to attack humans. I know you're just doing your job, but suggesting an owl could be responsible for Ollie's death seems like a stretch."

Big Ted's expression soured. "Hold on, I never said he was killed by an owl," he huffed. "I'm as open-minded as the next guy, but we need to explore every scenario, especially given the nature of the victim's injuries."

I noticed Evie roll her eyes. Big Ted had a reputation for jumping to conclusions, and the thought of him being open-minded was almost comical.

He turned his attention back to Twilla. "Young lady, you've given me a lot to think about. I might have a few more questions for you later. For now, I best be off."

I walked him out and watched as he marched toward Ollie's cabin to join his deputy, snow crunching beneath the soles of his pac boots. Somehow, I didn't think we'd done much to change his mind about the idea of a killer owl.

Evie waited for me in the great room, a sympathetic smile on her face.

"Don't worry about Big Ted. You know how he is. He gets an idea in his head and runs with it."

"I know, but there's no telling how much trouble he might stir up if he starts spreading rumors that an owl is to blame for Ollie's death," I replied. "If you think it's hectic around here now, just imagine what would happen if people think the primary suspect in Ollie's death is a snowy owl."

"On a more positive note, I might have a solution for our workload problem," Evie said.

"Yeah? I'm all ears." With the owls hunkered down in Beechtree, any offer of help felt like a lifeline. "What do you have in mind?"

"It's a surprise," she teased, checking her watch. "You'll find out soon enough."

Across the great room, Fuzz poked his head out from behind the kitchen door. He scanned the room and waved us over.

"Is he gone?" he whispered.

"Just left," Evie confirmed.

He stepped out of the kitchen, Charley trailing behind him. "What did he want?"

I sighed. "The good news is that Big Ted thinks he knows what happened to Ollie."

"And the bad news?" Fuzz raised an eyebrow.

"He's convinced Ollie was murdered. By an owl, if you can believe it."

CHAPTER 4

After Big Ted and his deputy finished searching Ollie's cabin, Fuzz and Charley got busy on their list of odd jobs. In the meantime, Evie and I made our way to the kitchen for a quick coffee break as we geared up to staff the front desk and manage the day's office work.

"Can you believe Big Ted?" Evie shook her head. "That man is something else."

"He probably thinks he's onto something, but honestly, he's more Inspector Gadget than Hercule Poirot."

The buzz of my phone interrupted our laughter. Fishing it out from the pocket of my apron, I glanced at the screen.

"It's Maddie."

A rookie forest ranger, Maddie lived in a cabin at the lodge with her girlfriend, Liliana, a feisty redhead who ran the High Peaks Hop House, a local brewpub. The two made an adorable couple, constantly on the go—and they were both going full speed this week.

Maddie and her fellow rangers were run ragged dealing with lost hikers and other emergencies, while Liliana was do her best to accommodate big crowds at the Hop House. To top if off, Twilla had taken up temporary residence in their cabin while she worked the owl info station.

"What's up, Maddie?"

"Hey Mom, did you hear about the guy who died at Hayes Landing? Is it true that he was a guest at the lodge?"

"Ollie Harlow. And yeah, he was staying was in one of the cabins," I replied.

"Well, fair warning," she said, "I heard Big Ted might be headed your way."

"Thanks for the warning, but you're too late. He's already come and gone." I summarized the conversation Evie and I had with Big Ted, and told Maddie about his theory that there was a murderous owl on the loose in Beechtree.

"Next thing you know, he'll have black bears locked up for loitering and raccoons for shoplifting," I joked.

Maddie laughed. "Yeah, that sounds like Big Ted. Listen, I have a crazy idea. Any chance you can meet me at Hayes Landing?"

"Meet you at Hayes Landing? Right now? I don't know, Maddie. Evie and I are swamped here at the lodge and . . ."

Evie yanked the phone out of my hand. "Your mom's on her way," she said and hit the end call button. "Don't worry, I've got the lodge under control."

"Come on, Evie. There's no way you can manage all those rooms on your own, even with the new cleaning schedule."

"You're right, I can't manage all those rooms on my own," she admitted. "That's why I called in some backup."

Evie explained that she had a connection from her days at the marketing agency, a client who owned a network of temp agencies all over the state, including one in Lake Placid. Evie reached out to her, and the woman promised to send a team of housekeepers to our lodge by noon. The best part? We could keep the same team on call every day for as long as we needed. And once the owl-watching crowd thinned out, we could decide whether to continue with the service or not.

"She hooked us up with a really great deal too," Evie added, a touch of pride in her voice.

After hashing out how we'd use the temporary housecleaning crew, I popped over to my cabin to slip into cold-weather clothes. Then, I made my way to the small family parking lot behind the lodge and fired up the Birdmobile—a Subaru Forester I'd outfitted for birdwatching and other outdoor adventures.

Cranking up the heater, I maneuvered out of the parking lot onto the snow-covered road leading away from the lodge, the Birdmobile rumbling softly beneath me. As I drove, my thoughts drifted to Maddie. She'd always been full of curiosity, even as a little girl. Without a doubt, she wanted me to join her at Hayes Landing to search for any clues that could help explain what happened to Ollie Harlow.

When I saw the sign for Hayes Landing, I turned onto a gravel path leading to a small parking area. I was surprised to find Maddie's SUV, covered in mud, sitting by itself. It looked like the news of a dead body at the owl blind had kept the birdwatchers away for the day.

I parked the Birdmobile alongside Maddie's vehicle, and stepped out into the cold, binoculars in hand. Looking around the airfield, I saw a number of tall poles spread across the open space, with snowy owls perched on top of at least three of them.

As I adjusted my binoculars, the scene snapped into focus. The snowy owls, with their striking white feathers speckled with black and gray, were still in their juvenile phase, their colors not fully matured. Yet, even from this distance, I could see they were almost as big as turkey vultures.

When one of the owls swiveled its head, its yellow eyes locked with mine through my lens. Seeing these rare and elegant birds in their natural habitat felt like a privilege, a reminder of the beauty and mystery of the natural world.

Reluctantly, I tore myself away from the owls and headed to the dilapidated blind situated at the edge of the field. Battered by time and weather, the three-sided blind offered an excellent view of the airfield. Yellow caution tape encircled it, designating it as a crime scene. Maddie was inside the blind, on the wrong side of the police tape, scouring the ground for any evidence Big Ted might have missed.

"You know, you probably shouldn't be in there," I called to her as I got closer.

Maddie looked up, shouting back, "It's okay, Big Ted called the all clear over the radio. He just didn't bother take down the tape yet."

Shaking my head in disbelief, I ducked under the barrier to join her in the blind. The ground was a mess of footprints, but Maddie drew my attention to a dark, ominous stain on the snow.

"That's where they found Ollie's body," she said, pointing at the stain.

I stared at the bloody snow. Poor Ollie. Cantankerous as he was, no one deserved to die in a bird blind. Then again, for birders like me, I supposed there were worse ways to go.

"Let's put Big Ted aside for a minute. Given what you know about wildlife, do you honestly believe an owl could be responsible for this?" I asked her.

Maddie chewed on her lip, thinking. "Owls are predators and incredibly strong. If a snowy decided to swoop down on someone, it could do serious damage. Maybe even crack a skull."

"Big Ted did mention head injuries," I said. "Maybe he's right."

Maddie scuffed the tip of her boot in the snow. "No, it doesn't add up. Owls don't usually go after humans unless they're defending a nest. But inside a blind? That doesn't sound right."

I agreed. "So, if an owl wasn't responsible, then Ollie's death had to be . . ."

"Murder," she said, finishing my thought.

We ducked back under the police tape and made our way back to the parking area.

"How's Twilla holding up? She seemed a little off today."

Maddie tilted her head. "Really? What makes you say that?"

"She was late setting up the info station this morning, which isn't typical for her. Plus, she had this odd expression on her face when Big Ted wanted to see the talons, almost like something took her by surprise."

Maddie tucked her hands into her jacket pockets. "She might have been late because she was out with friends last night. She didn't get back to our cabin until after midnight."

I threw my binoculars onto the passenger seat of the Birdmobile. "Is that normal for her? Staying out late like that?"

"Not really. She's more of a homebody like me," Maddie answered.

"Well, she bumped heads with Ollie yesterday morning," I said. "He really gave her a hard time about her work at the info station. Something about how she was encouraging hobbyists to get in professionals' way."

"I wouldn't worry about Twilla, Mom. She has a thick skin, and she's more than capable of dealing with people like Ollie," Maddie reassured me.

After saying our goodbyes, I slid back into the Birdmobile and revved up the heater. Now, I was left with even more questions than I had before.

Ollie's death didn't appear accidental, so what happened? Could it have been a freak owl attack like Big Ted seemed to think? No way. It felt more like someone had a problem with Ollie and decided to do something about it.

And then there was Twilla. Being late to work was one thing, but her weird reaction to seeing the talons? It seemed like there was more to the story than just a hangover from a night out with friends.

I felt a little better after talking with Maddie. She was incredibly sharp, which was part of what made her an excellent ranger. If something was up with Twilla, I trusted Maddie to figure it out.

For now, all I could do was focus on the daily grind and keep my eyes peeled for anything out of the ordinary. Sooner or later, things would start to make sense.

Meanwhile, I'd enjoy the little things, like watching snowy owls glide over a snow-covered landscape.

There was something calming about that, and I'd take every scrap of serenity I could find.

CHAPTER 5

Driving back to the lodge, it dawned on me that I suddenly had some spare time on my hands now that the temp cleaning crew was handling afternoon housekeeping. As I approached the lodge's driveway, I made a spontaneous decision to drop by the mercantile and stepped on the gas.

The bell above the door jingled, announcing my arrival at the mercantile. The mercantile's interior was packed with an eclectic mix of camping gear, hardware, souvenirs, and local crafts. Artisanal signs promoting fresh maple syrup and handcrafted fudge dangled above rough-hewn shelves laden with flannel wear, hiking boots, and novelties like forest-themed coffee mugs and raccoon bobble heads.

Sam was up front, arranging a display of books written by regional authors. When he saw me, his face lit up.

"Hey there, stranger. What brings you around?" he asked, his grin as disarming as ever.

"Just popped in to see if that famously bad coffee of yours lives up to the hype. Is now a good time?"

"Anytime's a good time for you," he replied, leading me past the counter to an office tucked away at the back.

I sank into a chair across from his messy desk while he poured the coffee. He'd warned me that the coffee was bad and wasn't kidding—it tasted like burnt beans steeped in tepid dishwater.

"How are things at the lodge with all this owl madness?"

I filled him in on the latest happenings, beginning with the Ollie Harlow situation, then segueing into my visit to Hayes Landing with Maddie.

I wasn't surprised that Sam knew about Ollie—news travels fast in a town as small as Beechtree. But I was a bit taken aback that he was also in the loop about Big Ted's killer owl theory. I thought cops were supposed to keep their hunches under wraps, yet here was Sam, telling me it was already the talk of the town.

"It's a shame about Ollie," Sam said. "He was just in here a few days ago picking up some hardware cloth."

"Hardware cloth?" Though we'd tackled a lot of the lodge's renovations ourselves, I was still learning the jargon of home improvement.

"Yeah, it's this wire mesh stuff," he explained. "Ollie mentioned he needed it to make shelves in his van. Seemed like an odd choice to me, but hey, he was in a bit of a mood, and a sale is a sale."

"Don't feel bad," I said. "He gave Twilla a hard time, too."

"Twilla, your owl girl? She seems really nice."

"She is. Ollie also butted heads with Mason Reed, another photographer at the lodge. I don't think he was very friendly with anyone."

Sam laughed, "It really does sound like you have your hands full."

"Understatement of the year," I said, picturing the pandemonium awaiting me back at the lodge. "I should head back. How about we grab dinner tonight and catch up?"

"Thought you'd never ask," he replied. "Maybe I'll even bring along a chocolate cream pie from the cafe."

∼

As I PULLED into the lodge parking lot, I groaned at the sight of news vans among the usual cars and SUVs. I had a hunch they weren't there for a heartwarming human-interest piece.

Inside, the lobby was swarming with journalists and media crews. A camera operator wrestled with a tripod in one corner, while his colleagues jostled for position at the front desk. If I didn't know any better, I'd have guessed Taylor Swift had popped in for a surprise concert.

Fuzz stood rigid behind the desk, his easygoing demeanor replaced by a bewildered expression. Even Charley seemed unsettled, perched nervously beside Fuzz, ears twitching at every sound.

Navigating through the chaos, I carefully sidestepped cables and gear on my way to Fuzz. "Don't worry, I've got this," I assured him.

"Hey, can I have everyone's attention please?" I shouted.

It felt like I was talking to a brick wall. None of the reporters even glanced in my direction.

Just as I was about to make another attempt, Fuzz snapped out of his stupor. "Quiet!" he bellowed, his voice sounding like a cross between a roar and a growl.

The lobby fell silent, and Fuzz flashed a triumphant smile before stepping aside, giving me the floor.

"Hey everyone, I'm Honey Palmer, one of the owners here at Loon Lodge. Unfortunately, we're pretty much in the dark about the man who passed away at Hayes Landing today. He was a nature photographer, and yes, he was staying with us.

But beyond that, we're just as clueless as you are. If you want more info, I suppose you could always try Googling him."

A ripple of laughter spread through the crowd. Apparently, my Google joke had landed better than I thought.

Then, a journalist in the front row spoke up. "We're more interested in the owls. I understand you have an owl expert on staff. Is that true?"

Maybe this was a feel-good story after all. Although the media's sudden interest in the owl irruption might might send another wave of owl watchers pouring into Beechtree, it felt appropriate to let the owls have their fifteen minutes of fame.

"Yes, we do have someone who's pretty savvy about owls on staff. And we're definitely open to sharing what we know."

"Awesome," another reporter chimed in. "So, about these owls—how do they attack? Is it the beaks or claws people should watch out for? Any stats on how many people owls kill each year?"

Fuzz and I were suddenly inundated with questions about predatory owls. We had to regain control of the situation before it veered completely off course, but Fuzz's bewildered expression told me he was totally overwhelmed.

"Hold on," I said, trying to collect my thoughts. "I just got here. Let me hang up my coat, and then we'll do our best to answer your questions."

I pulled Fuzz aside, out of the nosy journalists' earshot. "Where's Evie?"

"Probably in the kitchen," he answered. "Honey, these guys just sprung up out of nowhere. I was still trying to get my bearings when you walked in."

I asked Fuzz to keep the reporters at bay for a little while longer. Darting through the great room, I was relieved to see Twilla at the info station. After instructing her to stay put, I hurried into the kitchen to find Evie furiously mixing muffin batter.

"Evie, you're a sight for sore eyes," I breathed out, feeling a little winded. "The lobby's crawling with reporters, and they're all buzzing about Big Ted's killer owl theory. Maybe we can bring them back to reality with some hard facts."

I quickly sketched out my idea for a spur-of-the-moment press conference. With her expertise in marketing and PR, Evie was the ideal person to pull it together. In no time, we hashed out a plan: Twilla would lead with some owl basics, then we'd open it up to a short Q&A.

By the time the press conference finally got underway, the great room was packed. Standing behind a folding table at the info station, Evie, Twilla, and I found ourselves facing a mix of reporters, guests, and owl enthusiasts.

Evie set the stage with a few ground rules before introducing Twilla, who launched into a presentation on owl behavior, emphasizing their generally docile nature toward humans. She had just started to describe their feeding habits when a hipster in a flannel shirt and knit beanie interrupted her.

The hipster introduced himself as Tyler Barnes, a reporter with the Adirondack Daily Herald, the newspaper out of Lake Placid.

"I'm sure owl diets are fascinating, but let's cut to the chase. Could an owl have offed Ollie Harlow?" he asked bluntly.

Caught off guard, Twilla fumbled for a response. But the reporter persisted. "It's a straightforward question. Can an owl kill a human being?"

"Well, actually, it's not that simple," I interjected. "Owls are formidable birds, but they typically don't pose a threat to humans."

"So, you're suggesting there's a possibility an owl could be responsible?" he pressed.

My patience was wearing thin. "Listen, Tyler, owl attacks on humans are incredibly rare. Although it's theoretically possible, it's highly unlikely that—"

Before I could finish my sentence, the reporters were already packing up their equipment. Evie made a gallant attempt to corral them back into their seats, but it was futile. They had their headline.

As the great room cleared out, I spotted Twilla at the info desk, looking visibly rattled.

"Hey, don't let those reporters get to you," I reassured her. "They're just chasing a headline."

"It's not the reporters," she said, her voice tense. "There's something I've been meaning to tell you. I tried earlier, but you weren't around."

"I was with Maddie, then I stopped by the mercantile to see Sam," I explained. "What's going on?"

Twilla took a deep breath. "I think I might know where the murder weapon is."

CHAPTER 6

Twilla's bombshell about knowing the whereabouts of the murder weapon left me completely stunned. I just stood there, speechless, as I tried to wrap my head around it.

She reached under a nearby table and pulled out an old shoebox. Slowly lifting the lid, she revealed a preserved raptor foot, its talons long, curved, and menacingly sharp. "These belonged to a great-horned owl," she explained.

"Got it," I replied, though truth be told, I was totally lost.

Then, Twilla brought out another pair of talons, this time from a snowy owl, and set them on the table beside the first set for comparison. "See the difference?" she asked. The great-horned owl's talons were visibly larger and sturdier, with darker feathers surrounding them.

Twilla flipped over the great-horned owl's talons, exposing dried blood on the underside of the sharp claws. A dark red stain marred the soft pads beneath the owl's toes.

I leaned in, intrigued. "Where did these come from?"

"I have no idea. They just appeared in the exhibit today. I didn't even notice them until the police chief came by."

At least that explained the look on her face when she showed the talons to Big Ted. "This is bizarre," I said. "This has to be someone's idea of a joke, right?"

Twilla wasn't so sure. "What if that's actually blood? It could be Mr. Harlow's."

"That's quite a leap, isn't it?"

She shook her head. "Not really. The timing is too coincidental. Plus, old blood would look darker. I know it's wild, but these talons . . . they could actually be the murder weapon."

Everything Twilla said made sense, but if this creepy owl's foot was the murder weapon, what was it doing in our exhibit?

Twilla nibbled her lip. "Here's the thing. We have to keep this quiet, at least for now. Not a word to anyone, not even Big Ted."

"What? We have to tell Big Ted about this, like right now!"

"Think about it," she said. "If word gets out, it won't look good for the lodge. Big Ted's a wildcard, and the media? They're already making a circus out of this. Let's have a biologist friend of mine take a look at these talons. If it's human blood, we go straight to the cops."

I wasn't thrilled about withholding evidence, but Twilla's logic was solid. News of a blood-stained owl talon would send both Big Ted and the media into a frenzy, whether the substance was Ollie's blood or just stains from the long-dead owl's last meal.

"Fine, but if it turns out to be human blood, we're telling Big Ted. Agreed?"

Twilla nodded. "Absolutely." She slid the talons into a plastic sandwich bag and tucked the bag into her backpack. "I'll have it analyzed by my biologist friend right away. You'll be the first to know what he finds."

The press conference had left the great room in shambles.

While Twilla reorganized the info station, I gathered up napkins and coffee cups in a bus bin.

Afternoon sunlight streamed through the picture windows, blanketing the room in a warm, orange glow. Something about the light took me back to summer evenings, hanging out with Fuzz and Mom on the deck, playing cards as loons' calls drifted across the lake. It was a sweet memory, but it tugged at my heartstrings a little. I supposed feeling nostalgic came with the territory when you ran a family lodge.

Back in the kitchen, I found Evie sitting at the table, nursing a can of diet cola.

"There you are. I was starting to wonder where you'd disappeared to."

Evie looked up, her smile weary but warm. "Oh, I just needed a little peace and quiet after that press conference," she said, taking a sip of soda.

"I totally forgot to ask—how did the temp housekeepers do?" I asked, crossing my fingers that they might be the solution to our labor problems.

Evie broke into a wide grin. The temp crew had knocked it out of the park. Not a single problem, and they were actually looking forward to coming back the next day.

"I have news too, though it's not quite as upbeat as what you shared," I said, then proceeded to tell her about the talons Twilla had discovered at the info station. I described the blood stains and mentioned that they looked disturbingly recent. When I told her we'd decided not to tell Big Ted about the talons, she grew visibly agitated.

"Honey, I'm not sure about this. Hiding evidence sounds pretty sketchy."

I walked her through Twilla's rationale and eventually she came around to the idea. "You can tell Fuzz," I said, "but that's it, at least until Twilla's biologist friend determines if the blood is human."

After polishing off her soda, Evie tossed the can into the recycling with a clink. "Got any plans for tonight?"

"I do, actually. Sam's coming over for dinner, and there's talk of pie."

"Ooh, pie sounds amazing right now," she said, her voice tinged with envy.

"How about you and Fuzz? What's on your agenda for tonight?" I asked, trying to sound nonchalant.

Evie gave a tired laugh. "Oh, the usual glamour. While you're enjoying a romantic dinner, we'll be scarfing down tuna casserole and watching Jeopardy."

She sounded tense, so I asked her if everything was okay.

"Oh, it's nothing serious. Just a little spat with Fuzz last night. Typical relationship stuff," she explained.

I nodded my understanding. We chatted for a while longer, then I volunteered to finish up up in the kitchen and get things ready for the next day's breakfast bar. With that squared away, I took one last look around and decided to call it a day.

Stepping out of the kitchen, I saw Fred Caruso wandering around the great room, looking lost. He was bundled up in a thick winter jacket with a backpack slung over his shoulder, and I couldn't tell whether he was coming or going.

"How's it going, Fred?"

"Oh, hello there, young lady. I was just trying to muster up a cup of coffee."

"We've already shut things down for the night," I said, "but I'm more than happy to brew a fresh pot if you're interested."

He dismissed the idea with a gentle wave. "No, no, that's quite all right. I'll pick something up at the gas station."

"Are you sure?" I asked, secretly relieved that I didn't have to start the coffee machine again. "How's Lois? Is she feeling any better?"

"Much better, thanks for asking. She's lying down now, but we're keen to have her up and about tomorrow. Too much time inside makes us both a bit antsy."

I could relate. Aside from my quick trip to Hayes Landing with Maddie and my pop-in at the mercantile, I'd spent most of my time indoors lately. With the housekeepers on board, maybe I could finally carve out a little time to enjoy the outdoors myself.

"I hope the commotion earlier didn't bother you and Lois too much," I apologized. "It's been one of those days."

"I heard about the poor fellow they found at the owl blind when I was picking up our lunch. The lady at the cafe couldn't stop talking about it," he said.

Unfortunately, that didn't surprise me. The owner of the Beary Good Cafe, Wanda Rosenthal, was a friend of mine and the leader of the North Country Fly Girls, a local women's birdwatching group that Evie and I belonged to. Wanda loved a juicy rumor almost as much as she loved birds, and her cafe had a reputation as the epicenter of local gossip.

"The whole situation is just terrible," Fred continued, his expression somber. "And the man was staying here at the lodge, is that right?"

I nodded, confirming that Ollie had been a guest at the lodge, but kept the gorier details of his death and the recent discovery of the bloody talons to myself.

"It's tragic, really, but no doubt an isolated incident. Anyway, I'm off to try and spot some night owls, so to speak." Snickering at his own joke, he removed a pair of fancy binoculars from his backpack. "I picked up these night vision binoculars over in Lake Placid yesterday. Can't wait to see how they perform tonight."

I didn't know much about night vision gear, but the binoculars looked pretty advanced. "That sounds great. Let me know if they're any good."

"Absolutely," he replied, before adding, "Oh, and we're thinking of extending our stay for a few more days, if that's okay."

"You're welcome to stay as long as you'd like," I assured him.

Fred tucked away the binoculars in his pack and zipped up his coat. "Well then, I better get going. Nature waits for no man." With a friendly wave, he disappeared out the door.

As I finished straightening the great room, my mind drifted back to those talons. It felt like a case of déjà vu from last summer, when life at the lodge felt like something out of a mystery novel. Still, the chances the blood was human had to be slim, right?

Heading back to my cabin, I switched gears to dinner. Sam was due to arrive in just a few hours, and I hadn't even thought about what to cook yet. Then it hit me: a classic chicken pot pie would be just the thing, especially since Sam promised to bring a chocolate cream pie. A pie-themed dinner sounded like a winner to me.

Cooking wasn't exactly my strong suit, but I figured with a little assistance from the internet, I could pull together a decent meal. I mean, how tough could it be to make a pot pie?

CHAPTER 7

The smell of burnt pie crust hung thick in the air of my cabin. Cracking open the oven door unleashed a wave of smoke that left me coughing and gasping for air. So much for impressing Sam with my kitchen skills.

I grabbed a kitchen towel, pulled the overcooked pot pie out of the oven, and plopped it onto the counter, hoping a bit of trimming might rescue it. Thankfully, the salad and bread still looked appetizing, though I had to admit, they didn't require any cooking.

Once the smoke cleared, I took a look around the cabin. The faded couch, the stacks of old mystery novels on the coffee table, the quilt thrown over the armchair—it wasn't fancy, but it was mine and it felt like home.

Right on schedule, I heard a knock at the door. I opened it to find Sam with a bottle of wine in one hand and a chocolate cream pie in the other.

"Hey," he greeted me with a kiss on the cheek, then sniffed the air. "Something smells . . . burnt?"

I grinned. "I hope you like your pot pie extra crispy."

As Sam uncorked the wine, we filled each other in on the

day's happenings. He couldn't wait to tell me about the new batch of bird feeders that had just landed at the mercantile, and we shared a laugh when I described the terrified look on Fuzz's face as he tried to fend off the reporters.

I'd just started plating the pot pie when another knock sounded at the door. This time Maddie appeared, still in her ranger uniform.

"Hey, Mom. Just getting home from work, I figured I'd swing by to see if you've heard any updates on Ollie Harlow."

Whether it was the sight of Sam at the table or the scent of burnt pie crust, Maddie quickly picked up on the fact that we were getting ready to eat dinner.

"I'm sorry, I didn't mean to barge in on you guys," she said, sounding apologetic.

"No trouble at all," I assured her. "Why don't you join us? There's more than enough food."

Maddie hesitated by the doorway. "I don't want to intrude. Liliana's working late, and I was just going to warm up some leftover pizza."

The thought of Maddie spending her evening alone in her cabin, eating cold pizza, clinched it for me. I insisted she join us, and Sam sealed the deal by pouring her a glass of wine.

While a small part of me was disappointed about missing out on a quiet dinner with Sam, having Maddie with us felt right. Despite living just a few cabins away, it felt like it had been ages since we'd hung out. I quickly set an extra place at the table and we all settled in for a cozy evening together.

"How's work?" I asked.

Maddie dug into her pot pie, and a little gravy dripped from the corner of her mouth. "Just routine patrols for me," she said, wiping her lips. "But the ranger station is buzzing about Big Ted and his killer owl theory."

"I was just telling your mom how the whole town's

talking about Ollie," Sam chimed in. "Big Ted's going around sharing his owl theory with anyone who'll listen."

Maddie grinned. "He's totally sold on the idea that there's a deranged snowy owl on the loose in Beechtree. Everyone at the ranger station thinks it's hilarious."

I couldn't blame the rangers for having a bit of fun at Big Ted's expense. Under different circumstances, I'd probably be laughing right along with them.

"Wait until you hear this," I said between mouthfuls of pot pie. "Twilla discovered blood-stained owl talons at the info station today."

Maddie stopped mid-bite and stared at me, her eyes wide with disbelief. "What do you mean she 'discovered' them?"

I shrugged. "The talons belonged to a great-horned owl, and they just kind of appeared in the exhibit this morning."

"And you're telling me you have no idea how they got there?" she asked.

"None whatsoever," I replied and described the dark, blood-like substance on their underside.

"You said you were worried about Twilla's weird behavior this morning. I guess now you know what it was about," Maddie pointed out.

Sam looked puzzled, I could almost hear the wheels turning in his head. "You don't suppose those talons could be the murder weapon, do you?" he asked.

"Slow down, big fella, you're starting to sound like Twilla," I said, flashing a playful smile. "We're not even sure the stuff on the talons is blood. Twilla's having them tested by a biologist friend, but we're keeping it under wraps for now. I agreed that we wouldn't tell the police about the talons unless we're positive it's human blood."

I realized I'd messed up as soon as the words left my mouth. As a forest ranger, Maddie had the same law enforcement responsibilities as Big Ted. Inadvertently, I'd just dragged her into our little conspiracy to conceal evidence.

Maddie quickly covered her ears. "I didn't hear a thing," she joked. "For the record, the forest service advises everyone to fully cooperate with law enforcement."

Sam placed his fork on the table and leaned forward. "I'm not making any accusations, but how much do we really know about Twilla?"

"Well, we ran in the same circles at SUNY ESF," Maddie explained, taking a sip of wine. "We lost touch after graduation, but according to Twilla, she's been bouncing between seasonal field jobs for the past year—doing things like counting earthworms and oiling swan eggs for population control. That's about all I know."

"Time out," I said. "We don't really think Twilla was involved in Ollie's murder, do we? She's a good kid, a little quirky maybe, but I like her. And remember, Twilla's the one who told me about the talons in the first place."

"All I'm saying is that we need to look at this thing from every angle," Sam said. "Maybe she planted the talons at the info station herself, then told you about them to throw us off track, you know?"

"He's got a point, Mom," Maddie said. "Personally, I don't think Twilla's up to anything shady either. But we don't really know her very well. It wouldn't hurt to be a little cautious."

I felt my phone vibrate with a new text, so I quickly glanced at the message and started tapping out a reply. When I looked up, I saw Sam staring at me with anticipation written all over his face.

"Was that Twilla? Did her friend finish testing the talons?"

"Relax, it's just Annie." Annie Garza, the always cheerful receptionist and office manager at Beechtree PD, was another friend of ours. An avid birdwatcher, she was also a founding member of the Fly Girls.

I shared the gist of Annie's text. She'd overhead part of Big Ted's call with the medical examiner, and it didn't sound like the ME was sold on Big Ted's theory of a homicidal owl.

"Really?" Sam asked. "Did she hear anything else?"

Amused by his sudden curiosity, I replied, "No, but she mentioned it's been a while since our last Fly Girls gathering, so she's proposing we meet up here at the lodge tomorrow morning, after the breakfast rush. She might have more details to share then."

"I'm swamped at work tomorrow, but I'll fill in Liliana," Maddie said.

"Great. Annie's reaching out to the other Fly Girls," I continued. "It feels like forever since we all caught up, right? I'm really excited to see everyone again."

We broke out Sam's chocolate cream pie, and our conversation shifted to lighter subjects. Eventually, Maddie said goodnight, and Sam and I cozied up on the sofa with a blanket and mugs of coffee. I curled up against him, tucking my legs underneath me.

"You're turning into quite the armchair detective, huh?" I teased.

"Maybe I am. But who can blame me? Death by owl is interesting stuff!"

The conversation drifted into a comfortable silence as we nestled into our own little world. Wrapped in the warmth of the fire, the mysteries of the outside world faded away, leaving just the two of us to bask in the gentle flicker of the firelight.

CHAPTER 8

"Morning," Evie called over her shoulder as she mixed batter at the kitchen counter. "Coffee's on."

I made my way to the brew station and filled up the biggest mug I could find. The dark roast warmed my throat as I took the first heavenly sip.

Fuzz sat at the table, absorbed in his newspaper, while Charley happily gnawed on a bone nearby. "Sleep well?" he asked, his eyes fixed on the paper.

"Like a log," I said. "For some reason, I always seem to sleep better in the winter."

"That's a thing," Evie shouted across the kitchen. "I read about it last week. Has something to do with melatonin levels."

"Nah, it's the clean mountain air," Fuzz quipped.

I pulled up a chair, my stomach rumbling at the delicious breakfast scents. Before my butt even hit the seat, a voice from the great room echoed into the kitchen.

"Hello? Anyone around?"

With Evie on pastry duty, and Fuzz lost in the day's headlines, I volunteered to check it out.

In the great room, I found Mason Reed, looking every bit the wilderness photographer. Tufts of sandy hair peeked out from beneath his beanie and he had a small pack strapped to his shoulders.

"Morning," he said. "I thought I'd swing by to see if breakfast was ready yet."

"Sorry, not quite yet," I answered, "but I'm glad you're here. I've been meaning to tell you how sorry I am about Ollie. When I saw you at the info station the other day, it seemed like you two knew each other."

The easygoing expression faded from Mason's face. "You know, Ollie wasn't always such a jerk. He was actually my mentor when I first got into wildlife photography—taught me all the basics." A touch of sadness tinged his voice. "But then the photography game changed, and Ollie didn't. I think it soured it him."

Mason went on to explain how he and other top wildlife photographers had embraced new technology like digital editing, social media, and drone photography. However, Ollie had stubbornly clung to his old-school ways, refusing to adapt. As a result, he fell behind the competition, which affected his earnings. According to Mason, Ollie's jealousy had strained their once-close relationship.

I could certainly attest to Ollie's prickly personality, but Mason's insights explained the friction between the two of them at the info station the other day. It had to be difficult watching your protégé outshine you.

"I should get going if I want to catch the early light," Mason said, zipping up his jacket. "Take care!" With a quick wink and a smile, he turned and walked away.

∼

BREAKFAST SERVICE WENT SURPRISINGLY SMOOTHLY, despite a few hiccups. A guy who could have easily passed as Jerry Garcia choked on a danish, and the toaster caught on fire. But overall, it was the usual chaos, nothing we couldn't handle.

By midmorning, things had calmed down enough for Fuzz and Charley to hold down the fort while Evie and I slipped away for the Fly Girls gathering.

Wanda and Annie were waiting for us outside my cabin, huddled together like penguins braving the Antarctic. Ever stylish, Annie was bundled up in a heavy parka with a fur-lined hood, her long black hair hidden beneath a purple beanie.

Wanda, while not as trendy, looked snug in her fuzzy earmuffs, her wild curls pulled back into a ponytail. Her freckled face and ginger hair gave her a youthful appearance, belying her fifty plus years. Clutching her puffy coat around her, Wanda's teeth chattered as she urged me to unlock the cabin door before she started losing toes to frostbite.

I got a fire going while Evie brewed a pot of coffee. In the meantime, Wanda began foraging through my pantry. "Got anything to snack on?" she asked. "I could really go for a cookie or maybe some cake right now."

"Sorry, I'm fresh out. I don't usually keep many sweets on hand," I replied. Although, in reality, I had a few slices of Sam's chocolate cream pie stashed in the fridge for later, but I wasn't about to share those.

Wanda sighed, "I knew I should've brought some treats from the café." My stomach growled listening to her describe the lemon bars she'd baked that morning, especially when she mentioned their melt-in-your-mouth goodness.

The door opened and Liliana breezed in. "Morning ladies," she sang out, shedding her coat and boots at the door. "Maddie couldn't make it, but she says hello."

We all gathered around the fireplace, and Annie pulled out her knitting, the needles clicking in a steady rhythm as she crafted what looked like a blue scarf.

"Big Ted's on the edge of his seat waiting for the medical examiner's report," Annie said. "Though I get the feeling that he's not as convinced about his killer owl theory as he was yesterday."

"We told him it was a dumb idea," Evie snorted.

"It's obvious we're looking at a plain old murder, just like last summer," Wanda said. Then, pumping a fist, she added, "The Fly Girls are back in action, baby!"

"Easy there, Wanda," I cautioned. "Let's not get ahead of ourselves. This isn't like last summer. We need to stay out of Big Ted's way this time."

Evie agreed. "Honey's got a point. "You're right. As frustrating as Big Ted can be, we ought to let the experts handle this one."

Liliana fidgeted in her seat. "Wait a minute, let's think this through. The lodge, the cafe, the Hop House, the mercantile —we all have skin in the game, right? If Big Ted's owl theory catches on, we could get swamped with people wanting to see this 'killer owl'. And honestly, we're not equipped to handle another wave of owl enthusiasts. We're stretched pretty thin as it is."

"But if we can prove that a person, not an owl, killed Ollie, maybe things will get back to normal around here," Annie pointed out.

"Or as normal as it can be in the middle of an owl irruption," I added.

Wanda was practically buzzing with energy. "Let's start by figuring out who wanted Ollie out of the picture."

While I was wary of Wanda's tendency to get carried away, Big Ted seemed fixated on his owl theory, and it was high time somebody started looking for a human culprit.

Realizing this was happening whether I was on board or not, I decided to set some ground rules. "Alright, we can discreetly gather information, but no hardcore interrogations or anything risky. Just stay alert, and keep each other updated in our group chat. That's it. Deal?"

"Deal," Wanda agreed, though she didn't sound very thrilled about it.

After the meeting wrapped up, Evie and I made our way back to the lodge. We found Fuzz at the front desk, engaged in a tug-of-war with Charley, who was putting his heart and soul into it at the other end of the chew rope.

"Hello, ladies," Fuzz said.

"Hi Fuzz," I replied. Evie forced a small smile. There was an icy vibe between the two of them, and I got the feeling it wasn't going to thaw out anytime soon.

In fact, their strained relationship seemed to be teetering on the brink of a full-blown argument, and I was keen to avoid the fallout. Seizing the opportunity, I excused myself to check on Twilla at the info station.

"Hey, Twilla, anything new?" I asked as I approached the station.

She glanced up from arranging a stack of brochures. "Oh, perfect timing," she said. "Actually, I do have news. My friend finished analyzing the substance on the talons, and you won't believe it—it's human blood."

"Are you serious?" I blurted out. "I was convinced that blood came from the owl's last meal."

"I thought the same thing," she admitted, "but it's definitely human blood."

"And you still have no idea how those talons turned up at the info station?"

She shook her head. "That part's still a mystery, but if the blood is Mr. Harlow's, it debunks Big Ted's theory killer owl theory once and for all."

"How?"

"Well, those talons were preserved quite a while ago, and the the owl they belonged to has been dead for months, maybe years. If it's Ollie's blood, then someone used them to inflict those wounds on him."

"Okay then, let's assume the blood is Ollie's. Who would have planted the talons at the info station? And why?"

Twilla could only shrug. "I wish I knew."

"We have to tell Big Ted about this, pronto."

"Already on it," she replied. "I called the station, but no one answered, so I left a message. Is it normal for the police around here to let calls go to voicemail?"

"Well, 'normal' is a relative concept in Beechtree, but you'll be happy to know that the station does have a receptionist. Your call went to voicemail because she's in my bird-watching group, and we just finished a meeting at my cabin. She's probably on her way back to the station right now. I'm sure Big Ted will get your message soon."

After leaving Twilla at the exhibit, I made my way across the great room and stepped out onto the deck, gently closing the door behind me. Even though I was still bundled up in my parka, I could feel the crisp air nip at me as I leaned on the porch railing to gather my thoughts and take in the view of Beechtree Lake.

Big Ted wasn't the sharpest tool in the shed, but it was his investigation, and we needed to say out of his way. Still, the appearance of those talons at the info station nagged at me. It just didn't add up.

For the moment, I decided to enjoy the peace and quiet. One way or another, things would sort themselves out. I just had to trust the process and avoid stirring the pot.

Patience and prudence would be my compass. My North Star.

Oh, who was I kidding? I was definitely going to snoop around a little.

CHAPTER 9

*L*unchtime. Opening the fridge in the lodge kitchen, I found it crammed with breakfast leftovers. If I never saw another sesame seed bagel, it would be too soon.

With a little digging, I managed to scrounge up the essentials. Ingredients in hand, I assembled a pepper jack grilled cheese sandwich on sourdough, adding a thick tomato slice and a generous dollop of the spicy mustard for good measure.

The sandwich was unexpectedly delicious. The way the sourdough absorbed the tangy mustard and the juice from the tomato hit the spot. After savoring the last morsel, I wiped my mouth and hands, then carried the plate to the sink. That's when I spotted Fuzz's morning paper sitting on the old recliner in the corner.

I picked up the newspaper and sank into the recliner. Fuzz had moved it into the kitchen years ago, so he could keep company with Mom while she cooked. It seemed hard to believe now, but this kitchen used to churn out three full meals a day under Mom's watch.

Mom's cooking held a special place in my heart, and I missed it more than anything. Her breakfasts were the stuff of legends: fluffy pancakes swimming in syrup, bacon with the perfect crunch, and scrambled eggs so rich and creamy they melted in your mouth. She had a knack for transforming the most basic ingredients into a lavish spread. I still wonder how she managed it, especially considering the daily battle Evie and I face to manage a basic breakfast bar.

As I unfolded the newspaper, my eyes widened at the headline screaming up at me: "Beechtree Police Stumped by Killer Owl." The article didn't name Loon Lodge explicitly, but it hinted that the unfortunate victim was staying at a local inn favored by owl watchers.

Feeling a surge of annoyance, I turned the page, hoping to distract myself with less sensational news. My eyes skimmed over articles about a winter festival in Lake Placid, an upcoming fundraiser for the local high school, and other community events.

Before I knew it, I zoned out, lost in thought. Coming back to the moment, I checked my watch and realized I'd napped for almost an hour. Although my little siesta had left me refreshed, I suddenly remembered that I was supposed to take over from Evie at the front desk a while ago.

On my way to the lobby, I noticed the info station was deserted, with an "Out to Lunch" sign dangling from it. The front desk was also abandoned, with no trace of Evie, Fuzz, or Charley. Puzzled, I decided to take a quick walk around the property in hopes of finding them.

I pushed the lodge door open and was momentarily blinded by the intense sunlight bouncing off the snow-covered landscape. Once my eyes adjusted to the light, I noticed the housekeeping staff tending to the cabins.

"Hey there!" I called out, catching the attention of a tall woman with her chestnut hair in a ponytail and a burly guy who was all smiles. A young woman, earbuds in, was tossing a trash bag into their cleaning cart.

"Have any of you seen Evie or Fuzz?" I asked, walking over to the cart.

"Oh, Evie and Fuzz? They went towards their cabin a little while ago," the ponytail woman said.

"They seemed to be having a pretty serious conversation, looked intense," the smiley guy added.

The girl popped one earbud out. "Yeah, Evie was rippin' Fuzz a new one."

I didn't like the sound of that. While I was relieved they moved their argument to their cabin rather than airing it out at the front desk, the brewing tension between them spelled potential trouble for the lodge. Worse still, it put me in the impossible position of having to choose sides between my father and my best friend.

As I crossed the parking lot, my eyes landed on Twilla's blue Honda parked in its usual place. I had half-expected her to head into town for lunch, yet apparently she'd settled for leftovers like me.

The little Honda suited Twilla's no-nonsense approach to life perfectly. It was the type of car that didn't draw attention to itself, but it had undoubtedly proven itself reliable time and time again. Its worn tires spoke of the miles she'd traveled, and an assortment of nature-themed bumper stickers added a touch of flair to an otherwise ordinary-looking vehicle.

Wrapped in police tape, Ollie's camper van sat next to Twilla's Honda. Its earth-tone paint job and general appearance suggested that the vehicle had seen more than its share of road trips.

Faded stickers from national parks and wildlife sanctuaries clung to its windows, and it boasted a custom license plate that read L3NZUP—a clever substitute for LENSUP, which I assumed was already taken. The whole setup seemed appropriate for a seasoned photographer like Ollie.

I made sure no one was watching before I peeked into the window. Inside, it was a chaotic mix of professional equipment: camera bags and lenses strewn about, a tripod leaning casually against the counter. Though I didn't see any shelving, pieces of wire mesh and loose wires lay scattered on the floor.

Rather than pushing my luck, I went back to the lodge to cover the front desk. The ferns by the window seemed a bit neglected, and the entry mats were covered with winter grime, but otherwise, everything looked to be in order.

After watering the ferns, I retrieved my laptop to tackle some emails. Before long, I found myself doom-scrolling the internet, and it hit me that, for the first time in weeks, I was bored.

On a whim, I opened a new browser tab and entered Twilla's name in the search field. The results were meager. Her name appeared on a SUNY ESF graduation roster and a few social media profiles surfaced. It wasn't much to go on, but it was better than nothing.

Twilla's Facebook profile was fairly standard—photos of hiking trips with friends, party and tailgate pictures, the usual social stuff. But I noticed she hadn't updated her page in over six months. That seemed odd, especially for someone her age. Maddie and Liliana were swamped at work right now, and even they found time to post something every few days.

Her Instagram was a similar story, plenty of outdoor scenes and group shots. Once again, there was a noticeable gap of six months with no new posts. Something had changed in Twilla's life about six months ago, but her social media offered no clues about what it might be.

Maddie had said that Twilla was doing field research,

probably in areas with spotty cell service, which could partly explain the online hiatus. Yet, it still felt off to me. Twilla's generation was pretty much tethered to their phones, and they always found a way to stay connected, no matter how off-the-grid they were.

My phone buzzed, snapping me out of my thoughts. It was Twilla. Her voice sounded tinny and small.

"Hey, Honey. I'm sorry to bother you, but I'm in a bit of trouble. Maddie isn't answering her phone, and I could really use a ride. Can you come get me?"

"Of course, but are you okay? You don't sound like yourself."

"I'm alright, I've just had a bit of a rough day." She exhaled. "I'm at the Beechtree police station."

"The police station? Twilla, what happened?"

"It's complicated. I'd rather explain in person when you pick me up."

"Okay, I'm on my way. Hang tight." What had Twilla gotten herself into now? I'd assured Sam and the Fly Girls she was a good kid, but even I was starting to have my doubts about her.

I grabbed my parka and keys and headed to the Birdmobile. Driving to town, I prepared myself for what I imagined would be more bad news.

Whatever was going on, one thing was becoming increasingly clear: something was off about Twilla Jankowsky.

CHAPTER 10

I'd barely managed to squeeze the Birdmobile into a spot in the Beechtree PD's cramped lot when Annie dashed over. Her boots kicked up little puffs of snow as she jogged across the lot, and her cheeks were rosy from the cold.

"I saw you drive past the front of the station," she said as I rolled down the driver's side window, her breath visible in the chilly air. "I'm not supposed to leave the reception desk, but I figured you'd want to know what you're walking into. Big Ted wants to see you right away."

"Of course he does," I sighed, switching off the ignition. It seemed like there was never a dull moment when Big Ted was involved.

"When he heard Twilla's message, he drove straight to the lodge to grab the talons as evidence and haul her in for questioning. Didn't even give her a chance to grab her coat," Annie continued.

"Great," I muttered sarcastically. "I nodded off in the kitchen, and when I came to, the place was deserted. I guess that explains it."

She lowered her voice. "You didn't hear it from me, but Ollie Harlow's autopsy results are in. Cause of death? Blunt force trauma to the head. The medical examiner says there's no way an owl could inflict that kind of damage. It had to be someone strong, probably a man. And those scratches and the missing eyeball? All of that stuff happened post-mortem."

"After he was dead? Are you sure?"

"Pretty sure," she confirmed. "The ME thinks whoever killed Ollie wanted to make it look like an owl attack."

The thought of someone using a preserved owl talon to pluck out Ollie's eyeball sent shivers down my spine. It felt like more than just a random act of violence.

In fact, the whole idea of someone orchestrating a murder and then staging it to look like an owl attack struck me as something straight out of a true crime show like Dateline, not the sort of thing you'd expect to find in a quiet town like Beechtree.

"I have to get back in there," Annie said, quickly scanning the lot to ensure no one was watching. "Wait about ten minutes before you come in, so it doesn't seem like we've been chatting, alright?"

"Got it. Catch you inside," I replied, watching her dart off.

Stepping out of the Birdmobile, I began pacing back and forth in the small parking lot, snow crunching under my boots. My breath formed frosty clouds in the air as I processed this latest revelation.

If the talons Twilla discovered at the info station were the ones used to mutilate poor Ollie's dead body, then the murderer must have visited the lodge. Maybe the murderer was still there, hiding in plain sight as a guest. But which guest? And why would they bother leaving the talons at the info station, knowing they were sure to be discovered?

I walked aimlessly around the lot, occasionally stealing glances at my watch as I waited for enough time to pass for me to enter the police station. Just as I was about to head inside, I spotted Fred and Lois Caruso on the sidewalk across the street, strolling arm in arm, looking every bit the adorable couple.

Watching them enter the village pharmacy, I remembered Fred mentioning that Lois wasn't feeling well. I hoped she was on the mend, but I made a mental note to check in on them back at the lodge. For now, I had my hands full.

IT HAD BEEN ages since I'd set foot inside the Beechtree police station, and not much had changed. From the stained floor tiles to the flickering fluorescent overhead, the station looked as dreary and outdated as ever.

An unfamiliar deputy stood by the copier, methodically sifting through a stack of papers. He glanced my way briefly, then turned his attention back to his documents.

Approaching the reception desk, I found Annie engrossed in her computer work. "Hey, Annie," I greeted her, pretending that we hadn't just talked in the parking lot a few minutes ago. "I'm here to pick up Twilla Jankowsky."

Annie looked up from her screen, offering a polite smile. "No problem. Take a seat over there in the waiting area, and she'll be out shortly."

I slumped into a rickety chair in the waiting area and idly flipped through an issue of Time magazine, several years out of date. A few minutes later, the phone on Annie's desk rang. She answered, exchanged a few words, and hung up.

"Big Ted would like to speak with you," she informed me, motioning for me to follow her. "I'll take you to his office."

Annie led me down a corridor flanked by administrative offices. When we arrived at the entrance to Big Ted's office at the end of the hall, she gave me a soft, encouraging whisper,

"Good luck." I mouthed a silent "thanks" in response and lightly tapped on the door.

Big Ted's unmistakably nasal voice called out, "Come in."

Stepping into the office, I couldn't help but notice the meticulous organization of the space. Every document and item seemed deliberately placed. Behind the desk, Big Ted ruled over his domain from an imposing leather chair that dwarfed everything else in the room.

The entire setup seemed designed to intimidate visitors. The desk, made of polished dark wood, was a vast expanse with only a few items atop it: a nameplate in bold gold lettering, a tray holding neatly stacked folders, and a row of pens lined up with military precision.

In keeping with the theme, the walls were adorned with Big Ted's accomplishments. Various awards and certificates hung in perfect symmetry, each one framed and displayed with precision.

"Please, take a seat, Ms. Palmer," he gestured toward the chair across from him. I couldn't help but notice that my chair was positioned a few inches lower than his own, a deliberate move, no doubt.

I settled into the chair, my hands folded neatly in my lap. "What can I do for you, Chief?"

Big Ted steepled his fingers beneath his chin. "We need to discuss your friend, Twilla Jankowsky. I've brought her in for questioning regarding those owl talons found at the lodge."

I fought the urge to lash out at him for treating Twilla like a criminal, keeping my expression neutral instead. In previous encounters with Big Ted, I'd learned the hard way that letting my emotions take control was never a good idea, and I wasn't about to make that mistake again.

"As we speak, our lab is running tests on the talons to determine if the blood matches that of the victim," he continued. "Between you and me, I'm pretty convinced those talons are tied to the murder, which raises some serious questions about why they were in your exhibit."

He stared at me intently, waiting for a reaction. But I wasn't going to give him the satisfaction.

"I'm just as puzzled as you are," I replied calmly. "Twilla and I were both shocked when those talons turned up at the lodge."

Big Ted leaned back in his unusually large chair. "For now, Ms. Jankowsky isn't a suspect, just a person of interest. But she's on my radar, so I'd appreciate it if you could keep tabs on her and give me a heads-up if you notice anything fishy."

The implication that Twilla might be involved in something shady grated on my nerves, but I kept my cool. "You got it. If anything strange happens, you'll be the first to know."

He nodded, seeming satisfied with my answer. "Alright, Ms. Palmer, that'll be all for now. You'll find Ms. Jankowsky waiting for you in the reception area." Then, as an afterthought, he added, "And just so we're clear, I never fully bought into that whole killer owl theory. I was just keeping an open mind, you know."

"Of course," I said, though we both knew his explanation was a total crock of you-know-what. "I mean who would seriously believe an owl killed Ollie? That would be looney tunes, right?"

I found Twilla waiting anxiously in the reception area. She practically jumped out of her seat when she saw me.

"Time to go," I said, shooting Annie a knowing grin as we made our way out the door.

∼

OUTSIDE, I stopped and turned to Twilla. "I don't know about you, but after that ordeal, I could use something sweet. Can I talk you into coffee and dessert at the bakery?"

Twilla agreed, and we headed a block or so down Main Street to the village bakery. Ordinarily, I would have suggested the cafe, but the thought of Wanda eavesdropping on our conversation was more than I could handle at the moment.

The village bakery was exactly the kind of quaint and charming spot you'd expect to find in a small tourist town. Painted in pastel hues, the walls were adorned with photographs showcasing local scenery. And the display case was a feast for the eyes, showcasing a variety of baked goodies from buttery croissants to vibrant macarons.

Over coffee and cupcakes, Twilla opened up about her interview with Big Ted. He'd really grilled her about the talons, and she confirmed that he'd confiscated them as evidence.

"I'm pretty sure the lab will confirm the blood is Mr. Harlow's," she said. "You've got to admit, it was clever of the killer to hide the talons at the info station. With the constant flow of people at the lodge, it really muddies the investigation."

I swirled my coffee absentmindedly. "Hiding the evidence in plain sight? I've got to say, that's pretty brilliant. But it's definitely not doing the lodge any favors."

"I feel awful about the trouble all of this is causing," she said. "I wish I could do more, but I really have told you everything I know."

"It's alright," I reassured her. "We'll figure something out, just wait and see."

Twilla stared out the window. "We need to figure out who planted those talons at the info station before the lab results come back. If we can get ahead of the lab report, maybe we can spare the lodge some headaches."

I was skeptical. "That sounds great, but where would we even start? In case you haven't noticed, the lodge is like Grand Central Station these days."

Twilla's face lit up, and I could see an idea forming behind those bright blue eyes. "What if we round up everyone at the lodge who might have noticed something unusual? You, me, Evie, Maddie, Liliana, Fuzz. If we all put our heads together and share what we know, maybe we can crack this case wide open."

"That's actually a good idea," I responded. "It could help us figure out who slipped those talons into the exhibit." I chuckled. "Crack this case wide open? You know, you're starting to sound like Maddie."

She grinned. "I'll take that as a compliment."

"How about we have a girls' night?" I suggested. "I'll talk to Fuzz separately, though. Girls' nights aren't really his style."

The more I thought about it, the more I liked the idea. Who knew? With a little teamwork, we really might just crack this case wide open.

CHAPTER 11

When we arrived back at the lodge, I told Twilla she could knock off for the day and suggested she might want to relax at Maddie's before our girls' night. She was quick to take me up on the offer, saying she had some errands to run. After parking the Birdmobile, I watched as she hurried to her little Honda and zoomed down the driveway.

I found Evie at the front desk, idly tapping a pencil against her lip as she scanned a folded newspaper. Fuzz was conspicuously absent. Considering the recent tensions between them, that seemed like a good thing.

When Evie and Fuzz first got together, I had my doubts about how their relationship would impact the lodge. My concerns evaporated when I saw how happy they were together, and they'd been likes two peas in a pod ever since—that's what made their recent spat so confusing. Whatever was going on, I hoped they sorted it out soon. The last thing the lodge needed was more drama.

"Hey, Evie, anything exciting happen while I was gone?"

"Just the usual," she replied, glancing up from her newspaper. "I'm stuck on this crossword. A five-letter word for 'useful partners during a hike' starting with 'p'. Any ideas?"

I thought about it for a moment. 'Pooch'? 'Pacer'? Then, it hit me. "Could 'it be 'poles'?"

"That's it! You wouldn't believe how long that had me stumped." She laughed, crumpling the paper and tossing it into the trash.

Draping my parka on the back of a chair, I wandered over to the desk and leaned on the counter. "So, want to hear about my day?"

Evie perked up. "Something tells me I do. Spill it."

I told her about my unplanned detour to the Beechtree police station and how Big Ted had grilled Twilla about the talons. Evie agreed that we needed to figure out who had sneaked the talons into the exhibit, but like Sam, she raised the possibility that Twilla might have planted the talons there herself.

I admitted that the situation was bizarre, but I trusted Twilla. In fact, she'd suggested those of us at the lodge get together to trade information, and we'd decided to have a girls' night at my cabin. Who knew? With a little luck, we might even whittle down the list of suspects who had an opportunity to plant the talons at the info station.

Evie was instantly on board with a girls' night and had no objections to Fuzz sitting this one out. She said it would be nice to get a break from him. Grabbing her coat, she offered to pick up some snacks and a few bottles of wine, then promised to meet me at my cabin in an hour.

While Evie was out grabbing supplies, I took over at the front desk. My first order of business was to text Maddie: "Girls' night at my place, 7pm. We've got wine, snacks, and fun. You and Liliana game?"

Maddie texted back right away: "Count us in! Liliana's looking forward to it too. See you at 7!!!"

With girls' night sorted out, I shifted my attention to an email from a lady in Baltimore. She had booked a stay at the lodge and wondered if the snowy owls would still be around when her family visited in July. Seriously?

As I typed my reply, Fred and Lois Caruso appeared in the lobby. Lois seemed worn out, but Fred was as chipper as ever.

"Hey there," I greeted them. "How was your day?"

"Splendid!" Fred answered, cheery and bright-eyed. "We hiked up Sunset Ridge today. A demanding trek, but worth every step for the view."

I felt a twinge of envy, realizing it had been way too long since I last hit the trails. When I asked about trail conditions and if they'd seen any birds, Fred mentioned the trail was a bit rough and bird activity was minimal, just a few chickadees. He suggested I might want to avoid Sunset Ridge for now, and Lois nodded her head in agreement.

"Lois, I hope you don't mind me asking, but I noticed you heading into the pharmacy today," I said. "Everything okay?"

Fred laughed, holding up a bag bearing the village pharmacy's logo. ""Oh, Lois is fine. It's actually for me—I needed to refill had my sleeping pills. I just can't seem to get a good night's sleep without them. Though I've tried to convince Lois to give them a shot, she won't have it."

Lois smiled warmly. "But I do love the tea you leave out for me in the kitchen. It's perfect for those late nights. There's nothing like settling down by the fire with a great book and a warm cup of tea."

As they walked away, it seemed obvious to me that Lois still wasn't feeling a hundred percent. She looked exhausted, which wasn't surprising considering her ongoing struggles with insomnia.

I sent a quick text to Sam to call off our dinner plans, then answered a few more emails and opened my eBird app to check out recent bird sightings. With a little digging, I discovered that my fellow eBirders had recently spotted several snowy owls, a northern hawk owl and more than a half dozen species of songbirds at Sunset Ridge.

Fred and Lois were newbies at birdwatching, but they should have seen more than just chickadees today. Although I enjoyed chatting with them, I decided they might not be the most reliable source of information when it came to birding advice.

I was just about to close down the front desk when the landline rang. Seeing "Adirondack Daily Herald" on the caller ID, I muttered a quiet curse.

"Loon Lodge."

It was the irritating reporter from the press conference. "Ms. Palmer? Tyler Barnes from the Daily Herald. Got a minute?"

"Sure, Tyler. What's on your mind?"

He sounded annoyingly pleased with himself. "I have it from a reliable source that one of your staff members is a person of interest in the Ollie Harlow case. Care to comment?"

"Not really."

Undeterred, he pressed on. "Alright, how about we talk about the owl talons then. Don't you find it strange that such an important piece of evidence suddenly turned up at your lodge?"

His mention of the talons caught me off guard. How did he know about them? Big Ted just learned they existed a few hours ago.

For a moment, I toyed with the idea of telling Tyler where he could shove his beloved little reporter's notebook. Resisting the urge, I somehow managed to remain calm and professional instead.

"Lots of people have passed through the lodge this week,"

I told him. "Any one of them could have left those talons here."

"Okay, but this isn't the first time Loon Lodge has been linked to a suspicious death, is it? Just last summer..."

I cut him off. "We're done here, Tyler," I said and slammed the phone down.

The insinuation that the lodge was involved in Ollie's murder infuriated me. I didn't blame Tyler for asking questions. Of course it was weird that evidence related to Ollie's case turned up at the lodge. What really bothered me was that he seemed like the type of reporter who would distort the facts if he thought it would make a more sensational story.

I flipped the front desk sign to "closed" and put out the laminated sheet that told guests to call my cell in an emergency. Despite the day's drama, girls' night was shaping up to be a blast. Maybe we'd even inch closer to solving the mystery of who left the talons at the info station. Regardless, one thing was for sure...

If things didn't start making sense soon, Tyler Barnes wouldn't be the only one demanding answers.

CHAPTER 12

I tossed another log on the fire and stepped back to admire my handiwork. Interior design wasn't my thing, but I had to admit that I'd done a halfway decent job whipping the cabin into shape. It even smelled cozy.

The aroma of a spiced cider candle filled the room, blending perfectly with the fire's smoky scent. On the table, wine glasses shimmered alongside neatly arranged napkins and plates for snacks, while the soothing melodies of acoustic guitars flowed from the overhead wireless speakers.

Eat your heart out, Martha Stewart.

A muffled thump at the door signaled Evie's arrival. I opened it to find her standing in the doorway, her arms overflowing with a bag of snacks and an entire case of wine.

"I come bearing gifts," she announced, dropping her haul on the kitchen counter.

"I thought you said you were grabbing a couple of bottles?" I teased.

"What can I say, I got carried away," Evie said. She quickly poured herself a generous glass of Chardonnay and drank the entire thing in a single gulp. "Ahh, that hits the spot."

"Everything alright?" I asked.

Evie waved her hand, brushing it off. "Just Fuzz's antics. He decided to rearrange the kitchen layout, and we're butting heads about it. He just doesn't appreciate the concept of a good storage system."

"Well, he'd better straighten up, or he'll have me to deal with," I said. We laughed, but we both knew there was more to the story than a simple domestic squabble.

She quickly changed the subject. "Anyway, don't mind us. How can I help get things ready for tonight?"

Evie refilled her wine glass, and we went to work arranging an assortment of crackers, cheeses, fruits, and other goodies on platters. We'd just finished when Maddie, Liliana, and Twilla walked in, arms loaded with blankets and more snacks.

They dumped their stuff on couches and chairs, and Liliana made a beeline for the wine. Maddie eyed the spread of food and grabbed a slice of cheddar topped with a dollop of pepper jelly. "Great job on the snacks. I'm a sucker for a good cheese platter."

"Feel free to get comfy," I said, pointing to the plush seating by the fireplace.

Liliana and Maddie snuggled up on the sofa, while Twilla and Evie settled into the loveseat. "I swear, this cabin's starting to feel like my second home," Liliana joked, sipping her wine. "I've spent more time here today than at my own place!"

"Oh, right, the Fly Girls meeting was this morning," Maddie recalled. "How did it go?"

As Evie and Liliana recounted the meeting's highlights, the room filled with chatter. The main takeaway was the Fly Girls' decision to keep our eyes and ears open for any info that might help solve Ollie's murder. Then, I nudged Twilla to tell everyone about the owl talons and her conversation with Big Ted earlier in the day.

"Like I mentioned to Honey," Twilla said, "I'm pretty sure Big Ted's lab results will show that the blood on the talons is Ollie's. That means the person who left them in the exhibit is probably our killer."

Picking up where she left off, I added, "If we can figure out who had an opportunity to sneak the talons into the info station, then we can narrow down the list of suspects in Ollie's murder and hopefully get the police and the press off our backs."

Evie sat up, sloshing wine onto the cushions of the loveseat. "Alright ladies, time to get down to business. Who planted those talons?"

Liliana set her wine glass on a side table and leaned in. "Before we start throwing around accusations, let's start with the info station itself. Twilla, what happens to the items in the owl exhibit when you're not around?"

Twilla explained that it's illegal to possess owl talons or other specimens without a permit—and permits aren't easy to come by. The specimens in our exhibit were legitimately sourced, on loan from the biology department at SUNY ESF in Syracuse. In hindsight, she admitted that she probably should have secured everything in the office after hours. Instead, she'd just placed them in a plastic tub and tucked the tub under a table at the info station.

"I would have noticed if someone slipped the bloody talons into the exhibit while I was there," she said. "My guess is that someone snuck them into the storage tub at night. "I didn't even notice them until I was showing Big Ted the snowy owl talons."

Maddie plucked a cheese cube from the tray and tossed it into her mouth, talking as she chewed. "Okay, so we're pretty sure the talons got planted when nobody was around, probably late at night," she mused. "Anyone noticed strange comings and goings lately?"

Liliana shook her head. "I've been under water at the brewery, so I'm hardly ever here except to sleep. On the nights I close down the Hop House, it's usually past midnight by the time I arrive back at the lodge, and I haven't noticed anything strange."

"What about the guests?" Twilla looked around the group. "Anyone acting weird after hours?"

"I've noticed the nature photographers are up at all hours," I mentioned. "Including Ollie. He was always out late photographing nocturnal wildlife."

"The Carusos are night owls too," Evie added, giggling a little too loudly at her own joke.

I shared with the group that I'd bumped into Fred and Lois earlier, at the front desk. They both struggled with sleep issues. Fred had just refilled his sleeping pill prescription at the pharmacy, and Lois mentioned how much she enjoyed her late-night ritual of tea and reading by the fireplace.

"So, what you're saying is that they both have insomnia and wander around the lodge at all hours," Maddie said. "That sounds like opportunity to me."

I nodded but added, "Sure, they had opportunity, but motive? I'm not so sure. Have you seen them? It's questionable whether either one of them is physically capable of killing anybody, let alone an outdoorsman like Ollie."

As Evie reached for more wine, Liliana subtly moved the bottle out of her reach. Evie just shrugged and popped a chocolate truffle in her mouth instead.

"Getting back to the photographers," Twilla said, "I had an interesting conversation with one of our guests yesterday. She's an amateur wildlife photographer, and she couldn't stop raving about Ollie."

When Twilla mentioned Mason Reed, the guest said that

Ollie used to be a big fan of Mason's work, frequently singing Mason's praises on various wildlife photography forums.

However, Ollie and Mason's relationship had soured about a year ago. The guest had heard a rumor that their fallout was related to Mason's photography methods, though she didn't know the specifics. In any case, it was common knowledge among wildlife photographers that there was bad blood between Mason and Ollie now. "They have major beef," was how she put it.

Ollie and Mason's "major beef" wasn't exactly news—Mason had pretty much told me the same thing this morning in the great room. Yet, I was starting to get the feeling that there was something more to their rift than the professional jealousy Mason had suggested.

Evie suddenly snapped out of her wine-induced fog. "Figuring out who left those owl talons at the lodge is like trying to find a needle in a stack of haystacks," she said. "It doesn't matter whether they're staying in a cabin or a room, every guest on the property has a key to the lodge. Any of them could've slipped those talons into Twilla's storage tub after hours."

Maddie agreed. "Without more concrete evidence, pinpointing who put the talons there is going to be tough. We might have better luck tracking down other clues. You know, checking alibis, sneaking around—the usual stuff."

She was right, though it occurred to me that the usual stuff was exactly the kind of activities I'd cautioned the Fly Girls against.

As discussion about the talons tapered off, Evie lightened the mood with a hilarious tale about a guest who thought that spraying mouse urine on her beanie would attract snowy owls. Then, Twilla shared her own bizarre encounter with an elderly man who insisted on asking her oddly intimate questions about owl mating habits.

"Alright, time to call it a night," I said, noticing Evie's eyes beginning to glaze over again.

Liliana and Twilla volunteered to walk Evie home, while Maddie stayed behind to help with cleanup. After packing away the leftover snacks and gathering the empty wine bottles for recycling, I remembered Sam's chocolate cream pie in the fridge. I transferred the remaining two slices to plates, and Maddie and I dug in.

"Twilla came home late again last night," she mentioned, taking a bite of her pie.

I raised an eyebrow. "You still have no idea where she's been going?"

"Nope, but I don't think she's just hanging out with friends."

I took another bite of pie. "She seems honest, though. Like just now, when she told us about the beef between Mason and Ollie."

"I trust her too, but Sam brought up a good point at dinner last night. Twilla could have put the talons in the owl exhibit herself. It's a perfect alibi. And focusing on Mason and Ollie's feud? That just diverts suspicion from her."

I saw her point, but I wasn't ready to accuse Twilla of anything. Despite what I had advised the Fly Girls, it seemed like we had no choice but to kick our little investigation up a notch.

After Maddie left, I tidied up the cabin and started getting ready for bed. As I was brushing my teeth, I made up my mind that after the morning's breakfast rush died down, I'd finally spend some time in nature. And I had my sights set on Sunset Ridge.

CHAPTER 13

The clatter of dishes echoed through the great room as guests shuffled through the breakfast bar line, loading up their plates with pastries and scrambled eggs. Evie and I stood close by, cradling mugs of coffee. She looked exhausted, her eyes were swollen and red.

"Rough night?" I asked.

"That's one way to put it," she groaned. "I think I'm getting too old for girls' nights."

I gave her a sympathetic smile. "How about I make you my special hangover fix? It's made with a raw egg, a splash of Worcestershire sauce, a sprinkle of Tabasco, and . . ."

Evie stopped me short. "I'll take a rain check."

As the breakfast crowd started to thin out and the lodge quieted down, I looked out the picture window and saw the sunlight dancing on the snow. A perfect day for a hike.

Turning to Evie, I said, "It's gorgeous outside, and Fuzz is on front desk duty. Are you feeling well enough for me to sneak out for a quick hike?"

"Go for it," Evie replied, surveying the quiet great room.

"The cleaning team's got housekeeping covered, and I'm staying put. Enjoy the fresh air."

I was grinning from ear to ear as I hustled out of the lodge to get my hiking gear.

On the way to my cabin, I decided to see if Sam wanted to join me. I shot him a text promising it would be an adventure, and he quickly replied that he was all in. Traffic was slow at the mercantile, and his employee could hold down the fort for a while. Perfect. I texted back that I'd pick him up at his place in twenty minutes.

At my cabin, I quickly changed into my hiking clothes and filled a backpack with the essentials: binoculars, trail mix, and a thermos of hot tea. After grabbing my parka and gloves, I hopped into the Birdmobile and drove to town.

Sam lived in a quaint cape cod nestled in the heart of Beechtree, a snug two-bedroom he'd inherited from his parents. During the warmer months, he lived in his RV on a little plot of land just outside of town, but he spent winters in the house he'd grown up in.

I pulled up to Sam's house and shot him a text saying I was outside. In no time, he emerged from the side door and we began the drive up the winding road to the Sunset Ridge trailhead, a gravel parking area nestled back among the trees. The lot was nearly empty, just an old-school Subaru Outback with a roof rack and a Jeep that looked like it had seen one too many backcountry adventures.

The Sunset Ridge trail was a local favorite. It began with an easy stroll through a pine forest, then gradually ascended to a summit with stunning views of the surrounding mountains. Even with the snow cover, the trail appeared easily hikeable.

Around us, the forest hummed with the sights and sounds of winter in the Adirondacks. Blue jays flitted from tree to tree, their vivid blue feathers contrasted against green pine branches. Close by, a tufted titmouse with its distinctive crest hopped on the ground as it foraged for its next meal. And in the background, the steady thump of a woodpecker echoed in the distance.

I slipped off the binoculars from around my neck and passed them over to Sam. "Check it out, pine grosbeaks up ahead." I pointed toward a cluster of mountain ash trees heavy with fruit. He raised the binoculars and let out a soft whistle, admiring the rosy-breasted birds as they feasted on mountain ash berries.

As we continued on, the trail began to rise. I remembered from past hikes that it grew much steeper near the summit. Sam and I stopped to catch our breath.

"Ever tried the secret Sunset Ridge trail?" he asked.

I nodded, memories surfacing. "Yeah, I heard about it when I was younger, but I've never actually hiked it."

"It's kind of an insider thing," Sam explained, gesturing toward a faint path that branched off from the main trail. "It's a longer hike to the top, but the sights along the way are totally worth it."

The path was barely visible in the snow. Rather than ascending, it meandered downhill to the edge of a meadow. I stopped for a second to absorb it all—a wide-open snowy expanse framed by dark evergreens.

Before we knew it, the trail disappeared completely. Deep in uncharted territory, we navigated around boulders and threaded our way through dense patches of evergreen tree.

Eventually, Sam stopped and looked around, a puzzled look on his face. "I think we've lost the trail," he finally admitted. He was right, everywhere looked we were surrounded by untouched snow, no trail in sight.

"Looks like we're bushwhacking it from here," I joked, trying to keep things light. Sam wasn't amused. He just seemed annoyed that his secret shortcut was a bust.

Turning back probably would have been the wise choice. Sam and I were no strangers to the outdoors, but without a clear path to follow, we could easily get turned around and waste a lot of time regaining our bearings.

We decided to push on, carving our own trail through the snow. The forest grew more dense, the conifers' needles cloaked in a layer of snow. I took a deep breath of clean, piney air. This far off the main trail, it felt like we had the entire wilderness to ourselves.

Squeezing through two close-set pines, something near the tree line caught my attention—a small, dome-like object partially hidden in the snow. Curious, I moved closer to get a better look, Sam following behind me.

What we found was a cage made of wire mesh, cradling a motionless mouse inside. Around the cage were several thin wire loops resembling miniature nooses.

I glanced at Sam. "Any idea what this is?"

His expression turned serious. "Actually, I think I might. There was this conservationist guy who stopped by the mercantile last year for supplies to make something just like this. He said he was part of a team working on falcon banding. If I remember right, he called it a Bal-chatri trap."

"A what?" I asked, confused.

"A Bal-chatri trap," he repeated. "It's designed to snare birds of prey. The birds go for the bait, the mouse, and get caught by those wire loops."

I stared at the creepy device. It reminded me of a porcupine or hedgehog with those wire loops jutting out in all directions, but it was easy to see how it could entangle a bird, even a large one.

"Why would anyone leave something like this out here?" I wondered out loud.

He crouched down for a better look. "At the risk of

stating the obvious, I'd say someone's trying to catch birds with it."

The idea of any animal trapped in this thing made me sick "Well, we can't just leave it here," I declared.

"We'll take it with us," he said. "It's the only way we can make sure it won't be used again."

As he crouched down to dismantle the trap, I examined the surrounding area. "I don't see any footprints. If this was left here recently, there should be prints, right?"

"You're right, there should be," he said, focusing his attention on the trap. "But the snow hasn't been disturbed, and the mouse inside the trap is frozen solid. My guess is that it's been here for a few days, at least."

Sam made quick work of disassembling the trap. Freeing the last wire loop, he tossed the frozen mouse corpse aside, folded the mesh, and slid all of it into my backpack. I took one last look around before we headed back into the forest.

We retraced our footsteps back to the main trail. The thrill of our hike was gone, and neither of us had any interest in visiting the summit anymore.

The Jeep and the Outback remained parked at the trailhead, their owners still out on the trail. Sam and I loaded ourselves into the Birdmobile, and I cranked up the heat.

"You promised an adventure, but that was more than I bargained for," Sam said as the Birdmobile rumbled down the windy mountain road.

"Tell me about it. Who would've thought we'd find something like that out here?"

"You know, I don't have to be back at the mercantile for a while. Want to grab lunch at the cafe?"

Checking the dashboard clock, I saw it was almost noon. I could definitely eat. "Sounds like a plan. Maybe Wanda has some news about Ollie."

The moment I mentioned Ollie, Sam began rattling off

his thoughts about the murder. His ideas ranged from barely somewhat plausible scenarios to outright conspiracy theories. As he spoke, I realized that he was starting to sound nearly as obsessed and excitable as Wanda.

And I'd just agreed to bring the two of them together over lunch.

CHAPTER 14

The Beary Good Cafe bustled with a mixed bag of flannel-clad locals and Gore-Tex-wearing owl watchers, all of them eager to sample Wanda's famously hearty fare.

Sam and I snagged the last table, a quaint two-seater hidden in the back of the cafe. There was something about the Beary Good's atmosphere that never failed to cheer me up. From the framed sketches of local mountains and wildflowers on the walls to woven baskets and handmade pottery scattered throughout the dining area, the cafe's little details made it feel homey to me.

A waitress with electric blue hair and a nose ring materialized next to our table, order pad in hand. "Can I get you folks something to drink?" Her straightforward tone suggested this wasn't her first day. She'd been waitressing for a while.

"Hot chocolate with extra whipped cream, for me, please," I said.

"And I'll have the same," Sam added, "but can you put a cherry on top of mine?"

The waitress flashed us a quick, efficient smile. "Sure thing," she replied. "I'll give you a few minutes to look over the menu. Today's specials are venison chili, roasted beet salad with goat cheese, and wild berry pie."

Watching the waitress disappear into the kitchen, I suddenly wished I'd asked for a cherry on my hot chocolate. Too late now, that ship had sailed. I sighed, turning my attention to the menu.

"That Bal-chatri trap keeps nagging at me," Sam confessed. "You don't just find something like that every day. It's got to be connected to Ollie somehow."

I stared back at him with a blank look on my face. The connection seemed obvious to him, but I was lost. "What do you mean? I'm not following."

Then, he jogged my memory about Ollie's recent trip to the mercantile for hardware cloth, supposedly for shelving in his van. Sam wasn't convinced that was the real purpose.

Finally piecing it together, I mentioned that I'd snuck a peek inside Ollie's van. There were bits of wire and scraps of hardware cloth scattered around the van's floor, but nothing that even remotely resembled shelving.

"I can't say for sure, but there's a chance—a pretty good chance, actually—that Ollie was building an owl trap." To be honest, the thought had crossed my mind, but hearing Sam say it out loud raised the hairs on the back of my neck.

Our hot chocolates arrived, mine topped with a generous amount of whipped cream, just the way I liked it. I scored some of the whipped cream off the top with and took a sip, enjoying the comforting sweetness.savoring the sweet warmth. Meanwhile, Sam took the cherry from his drink and set it on my saucer.

"You have it," he offered, knowing my fondness for small fruits.

I smiled, popped the cherry into my mouth, and blew a

playful kiss at him. After the waitress took our orders, I leaned in closer to pick up where we left off. "But why would Ollie want to trap owls? He's into photography, not wildlife research."

Sam casually spooned whipped cream from his mug. "Maybe he wanted to get close-up shots of the owls?"

I shook my head. "No, I saw his camera gear, and he has those long zoom lenses like the rest of the wildlife photographers. He didn't need to trap the owls for close-ups."

"Plus, there are strict ethical guidelines that discourage photographers from interfering with wildlife," I continued. "All of the photographers I know take that stuff seriously."

"In that case, I'm stumped," Sam said. "I have no idea what he was doing with that trap."

"Got room for one more?" Wanda called out as she approached our table, expertly balancing a tray of food in one hand. Before either of us answer, she placed the tray on our table and pulled up a chair.

She could only spare a minute, but she couldn't resist stopping by to say hello. As she served us Sam's venison chili and my three-cheese grilled cheese, I noticed a familiar twinkle in her eye. I'd seen that look before. It was her "I'm dying to hear the latest gossip" look.

I was reluctant to tell Wanda about the owl trap and our growing suspicions about Ollie, fearing it would only add more fuel to the Beechtree rumor mill. Sam, on the other hand, didn't share my reservations.

"You'll never guess what we found at Sunset Ridge today," he blurted out. "One of those wire traps they use to snare raptors. We took it apart, but it seems like someone's out there trying to catch owls."

"No way!" Wanda gasped, nearly choking on her gum. She spat it out into a napkin. "Who would do such a thing?"

"We don't have all the facts yet, but—and please, try to

stay calm when I say this—there's a small chance that Ollie is somehow involved." I cautiously shared the details about the hardware cloth, emphasizing that Ollie might have had a totally innocent reason for buying it.

Of course, Wanda totally ignored my plea for calm. "You have to tell Big Ted right away. Trapping threatened species? That's majorly illegal!"

"Big Ted is out of the question. He's way too impulsive. I'm not even sure this kind of thing is even in his wheelhouse." I took a bite of my grilled cheese. "I'll talk to Maddie after her shift. I'll bet she knows someone at the Department of Environmental Conservation who can help."

I listened as Wanda and Sam proceeded to spin wild theories about the case, each one more bizarre than the last. Before long, I felt a headache coming on.

"Well, this has been . . . informative," I said, standing up from the table, "but if you'll excuse me, I have to visit the little girls' room."

I made my way through the busy cafe and almost reached the counter when a raspy voice stopped me in my tracks. "Hey, aren't you the woman from the lodge?"

Turning around, I found myself looking at an older woman dressed in olive green cargo pants and a well-worn denim shirt. Strands of steel gray hair peeked out from beneath her bright orange beanie.

"Uh, yeah, I'm Honey Palmer," I managed.

The woman flashed a gap-toothed grin. "Do me a favor, tell Fuzz that Wildcat sends her regards."

I wasn't exactly sure how to respond to that, so I just nodded and continued on to the restroom.

Back at our table, I found Sam and Wanda still engrossed in speculation about Ollie. Meanwhile, the mysterious woman was at the register, paying her bill. I nodded discreetly in her direction and whispered to Sam and Wanda, asking if they recognized her.

"Is that Wildcat Hayes?" Sam squinted in the direction of the woman, now making her way to the exit. "Yep, that's her. I think her real name is Shirley or something, but everyone just calls her Wildcat. She used to own Hayes Landing."

He explained that Wildcat's husband had set up a small regional airport after he came back from Vietnam, but it never really took off, so to speak. When the Adirondack Regional Airport had started pulling in most of the air traffic, it was the beginning of the end for Hayes Landing. Aside from the occasional private charter, it rarely saw any action.

After her husband died, Wildcat operated a flying club out of the airfield for a while. Apparently, she was quite the pilot back in the day. Then a few years back, she sold most of the airfield's acreage to a conservation trust, only keeping her house and a hangar at the end of the runway.

"You remember Wildcat's son, Shane, right?" Wanda chimed in. I must have looked confused because she quickly added, "You know, Plummet? From that thing last July?"

Plummet, the guy who ran the local bike shop and sometimes drove the only Uber in town. I'd crossed paths with him during last summer's mayhem with the mayor. As I recalled, he was a bit of a character, a trait that apparently ran in the family.

Just then the waitress with the blue hair came over to ask Wanda a question about an order.

"Shoot, duty calls," Wanda said, pushing her chair back. "Let me know if you hear anything else about Ollie's murder, will ya? And don't worry, my lips are sealed about that trap."

I promised to keep her posted, then watched her run off to the kitchen, narrowly colliding with a busboy.

Sam and I made our way up to the counter, where a

teenage cashier, clearly wishing he was anywhere else, took our payment.

"It's never dull when you're around," Sam said.

I gave him a sideways look. "I'm not sure if I should take that as a compliment or a complaint."

"Let's just say it's like riding a bike downhill without brakes, he said with a laugh. "It's thrilling, you just don't know how it's going to end!"

He gave me a peck on the cheek and continued on to the mercantile while I jumped in the Birdmobile and set off for the lodge. As I drove, I mulled over the morning's events. It felt like things were starting to spin out of control.

And there I was, pedaling along, with no idea how my brakeless bike ride would end.

CHAPTER 15

*E*vie was in the lobby again, engrossed in a mystery novel, her feet propped up on the front desk.

She peered over the top of her paperback, her eyes crinkling into a warm smile. "Hey lady, how was your hike?" she asked, marking her place in the story with her finger.

"Wait 'til you hear this," I said and filled her in about our discovery of the trap at Sunset Ridge as well as our hunch that Ollie might have had something to do with it.

She was caught off guard by the trap, but she agreed that Ollie's recent purchase of hardware cloth was weird. She also suggested that the person who set the trap probably had more of them scattered around the area.

I offered to take care of the prep for tomorrow's breakfast bar, but Evie had beat me to it. While I was gone, she'd baked several batches of cranberry muffins, and there were still plenty of bagels and croissants left over from today's spread. The bottom line? Tomorrow's breakfast bar was good to go thanks to Evie. On top of that, she'd found time to confirm all the new reservations and clear the lodge's email inbox.

"What's Fuzz up to?" I asked.

"Oh, he's around. He and Charlie staffed the front desk earlier when I was baking the muffins. I think they were headed out to his shop after I took over."

Back in the day, the shed behind the lodge was Fuzz's workshop, where he made a lot of the furniture for the lodge. Over time, as Fuzz's enthusiasm for woodworking dwindled, it slowly turned into extra storage space. Evie and I spruced it up for him and now it was his private escape, a man cave where he and Charlie could hang out for some male bonding time.

Following my chat with Evie, I decided to tackle some paperwork in the office. As I walked through the great room, I noticed the information station was unattended again.

Twilla was really pushing my limits. I'd stood up for her time and again, yet it seemed like the station was unstaffed more than it was staffed. We weren't paying her much, but technically it was a job and she had responsibilities. Where was she disappearing to all the time anyway?

Maybe it was time for a heart-to-heart. For better or worse, guests and visitors relied on us as their primary source of information about the owls, and she needed to step up or we'd have to find someone who would.

It turned out there wasn't as much paperwork as I thought, which was probably for the best because my mind wasn't really in it anyway. With nothing left on my immediate to-do list, it felt like the perfect time to see what Fuzz and Charlie were up to.

On the way to the shop, I spotted the cleaning crew rolling the housecleaning cart between cabins. The girl with the headphones caught my eye, and we exchanged a friendly wave. If budget allowed, I hoped to convince Fuzz and Evie to make the housecleaning arrangement permanent.

I made my way along the gravel path that led to the back

of the lodge, where Fuzz's wood shop was located. The shop was showing its age but it overlooked Beechtree Lake, and the view was spectacular.

As I stepped into the shop, a warm burst of heat hit me courtesy of the wood stove tucked in the corner. A generous pile of firewood was stacked close by, enough to keep the stove fed well into next week.

Fuzz's old woodworking tools hung from pegs on the wall, more for their sentimental value than anything else, and a couple of chairs were strategically placed near the stove. He'd even created a small nook for a dorm fridge and a coffee maker.

Hank Williams' "Lovesick Blues" blared from a CD player, while Fuzz sat at his workbench, his bifocals perched at the tip of his nose, skillfully winding thread around small hooks.

Charlie perked up from his spot by the fire and wagged his tail enthusiastically. I wandered over to give his ears a scratch before heading to the workbench to admire Fuzz's handiwork.

"Looking great," I commented, eyeing his collection of flies. "What are you working on now?"

Fuzz motioned me over to examine a small fly with brown and gray feathers clamped in the tiny vise. "This little number is a Hendrickson. No self-respecting trout can resist this baby, especially when the mayflies start hatching in the spring."

He clipped the thread and removed the Hendrickson from the vise, handing me the fly for a closer look. I turned it over in my fingers, marveling at the precision. The feathers were wrapped tightly around the hook, with just a touch of silver tinsel woven in.

"You still have the touch," I said. "I can't wait to see you out there on the river."

Fuzz chuckled. "Well now, don't get too excited. I ain't as

spry as I used to be, but it sure will feel good to make that line sing again."

I handed the fly back to him, and he gently placed it in his fly box, alongside familiar patterns like Adams and Elk Hair Caddis—his old standbys.

He placed his glasses on the bench and turned to me. "So, what brings you here? Just checking up on me?"

"Kind of," I replied. "But I also wanted to get your thoughts about something."

I shared the discovery Sam and I stumbled on at Sunset Ridge, curious to hear if he had any insights. Though he was familiar with a variety of traps, the Bal-chatri was new to him. We tossed around some theories, then I mentioned my run-in with Wildcat Hayes.

Fuzz burst into laughter when I relayed Wildcat's message. "That Wildcat, I could tell you stories about her. She's always had a bit of a soft spot for me," he said, mischief in his eyes.

A flurry of questions crossed my mind about the nature of Fuzz and Wildcat's relationship, but I wasn't sure I wanted to know the answers. So, to avoid a potentially uncomfortable conversation—for both of us—I kept my questions to myself.

"Ollie's body was found down at Hayes Landing, in the bird blind, right?" he asked.

I nodded.

"Well, there you go. Wildcat's a little quirky, but she's sharp as a tack. If something's going on up at Hayes Landing, she'll have the scoop," he said. "How about I take you to meet her?"

He was right about that. If anyone had information about strange happenings at Hayes Landing, it would be Wildcat. Even so, Big Ted had probably already spoken to her, and I doubted she would have kept any important information from the police.

"Thanks," I finally replied, "but Big Ted's on top of it. No sense ruffling feathers if we don't have to."

Fuzz shrugged. "Suit yourself. If you change your mind, you know where to find me."

I noticed Fuzz seemed quieter than usual. "Everything alright? You seem a bit off today."

"Ah, it's nothing, really. Just this thing with Evie."

My ears perked up. Even though I'd tried to stay clear of their relationship drama, I was dying to know what they were fighting about.

Fuzz went on, "You probably heard that we had a little spat the other day. It's silly, but I'm starting to think I'm too old for this relationship stuff."

"What do you mean?"

"After your mom passed, I never imagined I'd find someone again. Then along comes Evie, and well, she's something else." He got a faraway look in his eyes. "The problem is I've been out of the dating game for decades, and it feels like I'm fumbling around in the dark here."

"Fuzz, it's not rocket science. Just tell her how you feel. Or better yet, show her. Sometimes actions speak louder than words, right? I'll bet she just wants to feel appreciated."

"Show her, huh?" Fuzz nodded slowly, taking it all in. "Shoot, I just remembered something I gotta do." He whistled for Charlie and collected his things.

"Alright then," I chuckled, amused by his burst of energy. "I have to relieve Evie at the front desk anyway."

We left the workshop together. Fuzz and Charley scurried off to his pickup while I ambled back up the path to the lodge.

At the front desk, Evie had finally run out of steam and

was finally ready for a break. With gratitude for her coverage, I sent her to her cabin for some much-deserved couch time.

I spent the next few hours milling around the front desk, striking up conversations with a few guests, straightening things up, and watering the plants—until I realized they didn't need daily watering. The lodge was wonderfully tranquil. For a while, it felt like just another relaxed, lazy day in January.

While I was reorganizing the pens, I remembered that I hadn't talked to Maddie about the trap situation yet. Checking my watch, I decided it was close enough to call it a day. After dimming the lights, I put up the after-hours signs, and set off for Maddie's cabin.

When Maddie answered the door, she looked flustered.

"Oh, it's you," she said, slightly out of breath. "I thought you might be Twilla."

"Twilla? Why would you think that?"

Maddie motioned me inside. "Twilla's stuff is gone from the spare room. No note, nothing. It's like she just disappeared."

Looking around the now empty spare room, it was obvious Twilla had left for good. The bed was made, and not a single item of hers remained in the room. Wherever she'd gone, she clearly didn't plan on coming back.

Although her disappearance explained why she was a no-show at the info station, why would she leave without saying goodbye? I would've at least expected a conversation about her last paycheck if she was quitting.

Then, a more disturbing thought occurred to me. Sam, Evie, and even Maddie had all suggested I keep an eye on Twilla, but I'd brushed off their warnings, insisting we could trust her.

What if they were right? What if Twilla really was involved with the appearance of the talons at the info station?

Even more troubling, what if she was somehow connected to Ollie's murder?

CHAPTER 16

*M*addie and I nursed steaming mugs of coffee at her kitchen table. The layout of the cabin she shared with Liliana was identical to mine. The only difference was that their cabin reflected the decorating style of nature-obsessed twenty-somethings. It was a homey clutter of houseplants and wildlife art, with eclectic throws and cushions creating a laid-back, bohemian feel.

The centerpiece of the cabin was a large Queen of the Night cactus in a corner of the living room. A gift from Maddie's botany professor, the Queen of the Night bloomed just once a year, typically from dusk till dawn. It was a magical display that was easy to miss unless you were looking for it.

Maddie rubbed her forehead in frustration. "It doesn't make sense for Twilla to just vanish like this. I know she's been acting a little odd lately, but to leave without even saying goodbye? That's not her style. She's not responding to my texts either."

I stood up and refilled our mugs. "It's really odd. You'd

think she'd have given us some kind of warning. Do you think she might have said something to Liliana?"

"Nope, not a peep," Maddie sighed, her shoulders drooping. "I called Liliana at the Hop House, and she's just as clueless as we are. It doesn't make sense."

I tapped my fingers on the table uneasily. "While we're on the topic of things that don't make sense, Sam and I ran across something kind of disturbing at Sunset Ridge," I said and described the trap. "Sam seems to think it's something called a Bal-chatri. Ever heard of it?"

Maddie remembered seeing photos of Bal-chatri traps during her ranger training. They were complicated devices, not the kind of thing you could slap together on whim. Designed to ensnare raptors, they required the right materials, the right bait, and the knowledge and experience to know where to place them.

When I added that Ollie had purchased a supply of hardware cloth and wire from the mercantile a few days before his death, Maddie nearly fell out of her chair.

"Wait a minute," she cut in. "So, you think the trap belonged to Ollie Harlow?"

"It kind of looks that way. And Evie thinks there could be more traps out there."

"Evie's probably right," she said.

I shared that the timing of our discovery led me to believe someone was intentionally targeting snowy owls. Though Sam had floated the idea Ollie was trapping snowies for close-ups, we ultimately decided that didn't make any sense.

"It's possible Ollie was moonlighting for a university or a research group," Maddie said.

"What do you mean?"

She explained that universities sometimes get special permission to trap wildlife for research purposes. As a wildlife photographer working in the area, Ollie obviously knew where to find snowies. It was conceivable that he'd hooked up with a university or research organization that paid him to trap birds for a scientific study. If Ollie was experiencing cash flow problems, he might have been relying on research gigs to pay the bills.

"Researchers usually let the local rangers know if they're conducting studies that require them to capture wildlife," she pointed out. "I haven't heard of any research on owls or other raptors happening around Beechtree, but it's not impossible."

Shifting gears, I asked Maddie what she thought we should do about Twilla. Big Ted had flagged Twilla as a person of interest and I'd promised to keep an eye on her. In theory, I should tell Big Ted about her sudden disappearance, but I wasn't very keen on looping him in, especially given how loose-lipped he'd been with the press lately.

Maddie understood, but reminded me that murder investigations typically fell outside the rangers' jurisdiction. Though she'd help however she could, her hands were tied when it came to Twilla. And Big Ted, for that matter.

Suddenly, I realized who I should reach out to about Twilla's disappearance. I told Maddie my idea, and her face broke into a grin. I thanked her for all of her help and asked her to keep me posted if anything turned up about research projects in the area.

Leaving Maddie's cabin, I felt optimistic. For once, I knew exactly what my next move should be.

WHEN I GOT HOME, I pulled out my phone and scrolled to Detective Childress' personal cell number. A detective with the New York State Police, Childress had helped us resolve the incident at the lodge last summer. She also had the law enforcement clout to handle Big Ted, if it came down to it.

I dialed her number and tapped my foot impatiently waiting for her to pick up. Voicemail. With a sigh, I left a message, short and sweet, asking her to call me back as soon as possible.

No sooner had I hung up the phone than the front door flew open, and in stormed Evie, clutching a pillow under one arm and dragging a suitcase with the other.

"What did you say to him?" she demanded before I even had time to ask what was going on.

I stared at her, bewildered. "What did I say to who?"

"Fuzz!" she said in exasperation. "What did you tell him when you stopped by the shop today?"

I raised my hands to telegraph my confusion. "Nothing! I just told him about the situation with the photographers and Twilla. Oh, and I passed on Wildcat Hayes' greetings. Why, what's wrong?"

Evie flopped onto the couch with a groan. "Well, after your little pep talk, that stubborn old geezer went out and bought a diamond ring. An engagement ring, of all things!"

I was floored. "Um, well, congrats?" I offered cautiously.

She shot me a glare. "Don't congratulate me! Fuzz has been badgering me about getting hitched for weeks. I've tried to dodge him, but he's getting pushier. I guess he took whatever you said today as encouragement."

I led her to the sofa and sat down beside her. If she decided to break up with Fuzz, it would impact life at the lodge, but I felt sure we could work through the fallout. She was my best friend, after all, and I didn't want her stuck in a relationship that made her unhappy—even if it meant breaking my father's heart.

"Evie, if you think your relationship with Fuzz has run its course, I totally understand," I began gently.

She waved a hand dismissively. "It's not that. I'm as crazy about that old coot as he is about me. I just don't know if I'm cut out for marriage."

"But you've been married before," I reminded her. "Twice!"

"Three times actually. There was a weekend wedding in Vegas I never told you about. That's the problem—all of my marriages seem to end badly."

"And Fuzz sees it differently, huh?"

"Of course he does," she sighed. "He's old school and in his mind, if you love someone, you get married. He's got it in his head that I'm avoiding tying the knot because I don't think he's good enough or something."

Evie confided that whenever she saw an adorable couple like the Carusos, she pictured her and Fuzz the same way. If she agreed to marry him, she worried it would jeopardize the great relationship they already had.

"Marriage could ruin everything," Evie said, "and I'd never forgive myself if Fuzz turned into ex-husband number four."

I was head over heels about Sam, but the thought of him suddenly whipping out a diamond ring at this point in our relationship would freak me out too. Marriage wasn't completely off the table for me, but there was something comforting about just enjoying each other's company, at least for the time being.

"When he came home with that ring, I panicked. I told him I needed space, grabbed my stuff, and here I am," she continued.

"Well, it goes without saying that you can stay here as long as you need. It'll be like old times," I reassured her, "like when we first came to Beechtree and shared a cabin."

While Evie settled into the spare room, I quickly messaged Sam to let him know Evie would be staying with us for a while and that we'd have to skip our usual dinner plans tonight.

Hearing the soft blip confirm my message was sent, I wondered how long our new living arrangement might last.

And how many other surprises might be in store for me.

CHAPTER 17

I set my alarm to go off earlier than usual and woke up just as the first light began to filter through the curtains. Quietly slipping out of bed, I dressed and tiptoed past Evie's room. I could hear her gently snoring inside, no doubt cozy and snug beneath a mountain of blankets.

In the kitchen, I scribbled a quick note and left it on the table for her:

"Morning Evie! I'm taking care of the breakfast bar, so enjoy a morning off. You deserve it. Catch you at lunch! - Honey"

On my way into the lodge, I grabbed some firewood from the pile outside and arranged them in the fireplace, leaving plenty of space for airflow. With a flick of a match, I lit the kindling and watched as the fire slowly grew, casting a warm glow around the room.

Next, I began artfully arranging Evie's cranberry muffins on a serving tray. Her muffins were always a hit, and would no doubt be one of the first items we ran out of. Along with the muffins, I laid out an assortment of pastries, added some fresh fruit for color, a few types of yogurt, and granola for those who like a bit of crunch.

By the time the early birds wandered in, the fire was roaring and the breakfast bar was all set up and ready to go, offering a warm welcome and a tasty start to the day.

The morning unfolded without a hitch. Guests streamed in and out at a brisk pace, and everyone left with smiles on their faces. As I was refilling the coffee urns, a group of middle-aged women breezed into the great room. I recognized them as the rowdy birding club staying in Cabin 4.

The group made a beeline for the breakfast bar, ooh-ing and ahh-ing over the baked goods. One lady piled her plate perilously high with muffins and croissants, while another grabbed a stack of napkins and began to fold them into origami birds at their tables.

"Hope you ladies are enjoying everything," I said as I approached their table a little while later. "How are those muffins treating you?"

"The muffins were delicious," one of them replied, popping a grape into her mouth. "We've got a big hike planned today, so we're loading up on carbs."

As the birders finished their breakfast and set off for their hike, another guest approached me. "Hey, do you know what time the information station opens today? We're hoping to get some pointers on finding those owls."

I stifled a groan. With Twilla gone, the info station was unstaffed yet again.

"Unfortunately, the station's closed today," I told him, trying to mask my irritation. I could see the disappointment on his face, so I offered him a few suggestions on the best spots for owl sightings, and assured him he had a great chance of spotting an owl or two.

As he walked away, my eyes drifted to the empty info station. I couldn't get Twilla out of my mind. Why did she leave like that, without saying a word? Even worse, what if she really was connected to Ollie's murder?

The breakfast rush died down, and I spotted Mason Reed sitting alone at a table finishing his meal. I grabbed a coffee and asked if I could join him.

"Be my guest," he said through a mouthful of bagel.

I pulled out the chair across from him and sat down. "What's on your agenda today?" I asked, taking a sip of coffee.

Mason washed down the bagel with a big slurp of orange juice. "I'm hoping to capture a few more shots of the owls before they're gone. It looks like their numbers are dwindling, and I doubt they'll be around much longer."

Several other guests had also mentioned they weren't seeing as many owls lately. If the irruption really was winding down, then the crowds of owl watchers would soon leave Beechtree en masse—giving Ollie's killer a perfect opportunity to slip away unnoticed.

If that happened, it spelled bad news for the lodge. Between Big Ted's suspicions about Twilla and Tyler Barnes' not-so-subtle insinuations, the lodge would forever be associated with an unsolved murder.

I didn't really think Mason was responsible for Ollie's death, but their rocky relationship was hard to ignore. It dawned on me this might be a good opportunity to get some answers.

I decided to ease into it. "So, Mason, how are you holding up? About Ollie, I mean."

He stared into his glass of OJ. "It's strange thinking I won't run into him anymore, but I'm getting by," he confessed. Then he looked up at me. "Heard any news from the police?"

"Not much," I said, bending the truth a bit. It didn't seem like a good idea to share too many details with someone who was technically a suspect. "They're probably still collecting evidence, verifying alibis, the typical stuff. By the way, has Big Ted asked you about your whereabouts when Ollie . . . you know?" I asked, trying to keep it light and casual.

Mason squirmed in his chair. "They talked to me. I told Big Ted's deputy that I was out taking night shots," he said, but there was something off about his tone.

"Really? Someone was just asking me about good spots for night photography." That was an outright lie, but I wanted details. "Where did you go?"

"I managed to get some decent shots, but to be honest, I can't recall the exact place. I've been to so many spots this week; they've all started to blend together," he said, visibly tense. Suddenly, he got up from his chair. "I should go if I want to catch the morning light," he said, hastily making his exit..

Well, that was weird. I'd definitely struck a nerve when I asked Mason where he was the night of Ollie's murder. One minute he was all cool and collected, and the next, he was practically racing for the door.

I wasn't sure what to make of it yet, but Mason Reed had just moved up to the top of my list of suspects.

I SETTLED into my squeaky office chair and fired up my laptop, fully intending to knock out the day's admin tasks before Evie showed up for lunch. However, I couldn't stop thinking about Mason. Something about him didn't seem right.

Instead of tackling office work, I found myself opening a browser and typing "Mason Reed" in the search bar. I wasn't sure what I was looking for, but the results seemed fairly standard for a semi-famous wildlife photographer.

In addition to his photo galleries, I ran across several articles celebrating his achievements as well as interviews in which Mason shared his passion for capturing nature's raw beauty and talked about his excursions to far-flung places.

Mason's social media presence didn't offer any groundbreaking insights either. His pages were a mix of his professional shots and personal moments, all captured in his distinctive photographic style. He really had a gift for making even the most ordinary scenes pop visually. His professional photos were particularly striking, each one telling a part of his story and showcasing his evolution as an outdoor photographer.

On the personal side, his social media pages featured snapshots of friends and the occasional behind-the-scenes look at his photography projects. It felt like a glimpse into his life—or at least a curated version of it.

He'd managed to cultivate a pretty impressive social following. People didn't just passively scroll through the stuff he posted. They interacted with it, with comments ranging from admiration of his artistic eye to curiosity about his techniques.

I was about to give up when I remembered something Twilla said at girls' night. She'd mentioned a discussion she had with one of the guests about Mason. The guest had hinted that the bad blood between Ollie and Mason ran deeper than Mason had implied. She'd also said that their rivalry was common knowledge in wildlife photography circles.

On a hunch, I started poking around several online photography forums and message boards. Amid the usual mix of gear talk, photo critiques, and people planning meetups, I found a thread that caught my eye: "Mason Reed - Ethical Concerns?"

The thread was a heated debate about some of Mason's

award-winning photographs. A few users, especially one named L3NZUP, were calling him out for unethical post-processing and possibly using AI to create composite images. L3NZUP even pointed out specific instances where the lighting and angles didn't match up.

Some of the technical details went over my head, but the more I read L3NZUP's detailed posts, the more I became convinced that Mason was a fraud. L3NZUP ... where had I seen that name before. Then it dawned on me. L3NZUP was the custom license plate on Ollie's camper van.

The outspoken user had to be be Ollie. Judging by the dates, he'd been voicing concerns about Mason's work for months, and his arguments were starting to gain traction among other photographers.

I settled deeper into my chair as the pieces started to fall into place. Ollie and Mason's feud wasn't a simple case of professional jealousy or a personal grudge. It was about survival in a cutthroat industry, where a person's reputation could make or break their career.

When it came down to it, Ollie wasn't just criticizing Mason's work—he was threatening Mason's entire livelihood. The question now wasn't whether Mason had a motive to want Ollie out of the picture, but how far he might have gone to protect his career.

CHAPTER 18

*E*ventually, I got around to tackling the day's office tasks. After pouring myself another cup of coffee, I hunkered down at the computer to slog through emails and log new reservations into the system.

One of the emails was from a returning guest who was asking about availability for a weekend getaway in February. I typed a friendly reply, confirming that we had plenty of vacancies that weekend and we'd be delighted to host her and her husband again. Hopefully things would settle down around here by then.

Another email popped up from someone who'd visited us last summer. He wondered if it would be possible to organize a small family reunion here at the lodge. I responded enthusiastically, explaining the various accommodations we could offer and suggesting some fun activities for their group. Lately, there had been a surge in reservation requests from repeat guests, and I saw it as a positive sign that the updates we'd made to the lodge—not to mention Evie's killer marketing campaigns—were hitting the mark.

I whipped through the office duties faster than usual, and

by midmorning, I was all caught up. Earlier, when I was closing the breakfast bar, I'd noticed Fuzz and Charley at the front desk. Even though it wasn't quite time for a shift change yet, I decided I could go out there and relieve Fuzz a bit early.

As I was shutting down my laptop, I got a text from Sam, asking me to meet him at the mercantile. Curious, I texted back to ask why, but all I got was a mysterious "I'll tell you when you get here." A few elusive messages later, he managed to persuade me to make the trip into town, assuring me that it was something important.

I gave Fuzz a heads-up that I was heading out to meet Sam and would be back shortly. He told me not to fret, he and Charley had everything at the lodge under control. Grabbing my parka, I headed out to the Birdmobile, curious —and a little concerned—about why Sam was acting so secretive.

I found him at his usual spot, standing at the register behind the mercantile's counter. His expression brightened when he saw me, and he gestured me forward. The moment I reached the counter, he took my hand and led me toward his office at the back of the store. I got the impression from his brisk stride that whatever was waiting for me, it involved more than a bad cup of coffee.

Stepping into the office, I was met by a fit, middle-aged woman clad in a black parka with faux fur lining the collar. She had her hair pulled back in a no-nonsense ponytail, and a rather large gun holstered at her hip. Detective Childress.

And standing right beside her was Twilla, beaming from ear to ear.

I was flabbergasted. The last thing I'd expected to find in Sam's office was Twilla, let alone a state police detective. Before I could process what was happening, Childress moved in for a big, warm hug. "Good to see you again, Honey." Twilla flashed me a little wave.

Sam quickly excused himself, muttering something about giving us space. The three of us settled around the desk, and I turned to Childress. "Nice to see you too, but what's this all about?"

Childress sighed. "It's a little complicated." She explained that she received my message, but wanted to talk to me in person and couldn't meet me at the lodge because it was too risky. So, she arranged with Sam to meet in his office, and she and Twilla had sneaked in through the back to stay under the radar.

The cloak-and-dagger routine seemed a bit over the top. After all, this was Beechtree, not East Berlin. Childress must have noticed my confusion because she held up a hand to explain.

"Let's start at the beginning," she said. "Over the past year, the state police and the Department of Environmental Conservation have been joining forces to dismantle a wildlife trafficking ring across the state. When the snowy owl irruption hit, the operation shifted its focus to Beechtree."

"Wildlife trafficking? You mean there are actually people out there buying and selling snowy owls?"

Twilla finally joined the conversation. "You'd be surprised. Snowy owls are a hot commodity in the trafficking world. Collectors and even some zoos have always wanted them. But ever since the Harry Potter series hit the shelves, the demand for these owls has skyrocketed. These days, a single bird can go for as much as $20,000."

She went on to explain how the illegal wildlife trade is a major threat to the species. "The irony is that snowies make terrible pets," Twilla said. "They need special food, lots of space, and they live for more than twenty years. People think they're getting a Hedwig for the kids, only to discover they're too much to handle. Sanctuaries are full of owls that are lucky enough to get rescued, but a lot of trafficked birds aren't so fortunate."

"And how do you fit into all this?" I asked.

Twilla shifted in her chair. "I need to come clean about something. When I first showed up at the lodge, I wasn't completely upfront with you. After graduating from SUNY ESF, I became an undercover investigator with the DEC. I was deep into this wildlife trafficking case when the snowy owl situation hit, so I used my connection with Maddie to land the job at the info station. Our task force believed it was only a matter of time before the traffickers would show up at the lodge."

I had to acknowledge the cleverness of their strategy. If traffickers needed intel on owl sightings, our info station was probably one of the first places they'd look.

"Maddie's in the loop on all of this, right?" I asked. Given her role as a ranger, I figured Maddie must be privy to any wildlife-related law enforcement operations in the area.

Twilla shook her head. "Not in the slightest. I fed her the same line I gave you—that I'm just a wildlife educator looking for work. However, I've been sneaking off at night to meet with my task force, and I'm starting to think Maddie's getting wise to the fact there's more to my story."

I acknowledged that Twilla's unexplained disappearances hadn't gone unnoticed by Maddie and me. We'd shared our concerns with Evie and Sam, but beyond our little circle, no one at the lodge suspected Twilla was more than she seemed.

Just as I was about to ask Twilla if her work at the lodge had turned up anything, Childress cut in. "We suspect that one of the traffickers might be posing as a guest or visitor at your lodge. That's why we couldn't meet you there. If a state police detective suddenly showed up, it could scare them off. We couldn't risk it."

"What makes you think traffickers are staying at the lodge?"

Twilla leaned in. "Because Ollie Harlow was a trafficker. We've had our eye on him for a while, and we know he was working with an accomplice. Our current theory is that this person is still at the lodge, probably trying to tie up loose ends and cover their tracks."

I slumped back in my chair. Ollie was a wildlife trafficker. I told Childress and Twilla about the trap Sam and I found at Sunset Ridge and why we suspected Ollie might have put it there. His motivation for buying the hardware cloth finally made sense, but the thought of unwittingly hosting a wildlife trafficker at our lodge turned my stomach.

"Okay, I hear what you're saying," I said, "but Twilla, what about the bloody talons you found in the exhibit? And if you're so sure Ollie's partner is still at the lodge, why did you just disappear like that?"

"I honestly have no idea how those talons ended up in the exhibit," Twilla said. "Remember when I said I was having them tested by a friend?" I nodded. "Well, my 'friend' was the state police lab. They're the ones who determined that the blood on the talons was human."

Childress explained that Beechtree PD's latest lab results were also in, confirming that the blood on the talons was Ollie's. And as usual, Big Ted immediately jumped to the wrong conclusion and was gearing up to arrest Twilla for Ollie's murder.

The DEC could have just notified Big Ted that Twilla was part of a task force, but they were wary since Big Ted had a reputation for being a bit too talkative with the press. If word leaked that the lodge's owl expert was with the DEC, Ollie's accomplice would be gone in a flash.

"Which brings us to why we're having this conversation," Childress continued. "With Twilla sidelined, we need someone at Loon Lodge to be our eyes and ears. Believe it or not, you might just be our best shot at catching Ollie's partner."

Running a lodge in the Adirondacks, I expected curveballs, but I never imagined I'd be involved in something like this. The thought of doing anything close to undercover work seemed totally out of my league. I was used to managing reservations and breakfast service, not solving murders and investigating wildlife traffickers. Yet here I was, faced with the prospect of running a covert op at my own lodge.

Twilla's face grew serious. "There's just one thing," she said. "You have to keep all of this completely secret. Don't mention a word to anyone, not Fuzz, Evie, nobody. And you have to act clueless when Big Ted shows up to arrest me, which will probably happen later today."

Childress nodded in agreement. "Keeping the accomplice in the dark about your involvement is key. I don't want to scare you, but your safety could be at risk. Just keep a low profile, stay observant, and report back to us."

She stared me in the eye. "So Honey, do you think can handle this?"

"Do I really have a choice?"

She shook her head. "Not if we want to get to the bottom of this."

I took a deep breath. This was uncharted territory, and the weight of it suddenly felt very real.

"Okay, I'm in," I said, silently praying I wouldn't regret it.

CHAPTER 19

The door closed softly behind them, leaving me alone in Sam's office. I collapsed into his chair, my mind reeling with everything Childress and Twilla had just laid on me.

A wildlife trafficking ring, operating right under our noses in Beechtree. Ollie, a respected nature photographer, trapping owls to sell on the black market. And Twilla, Maddie's college friend, working undercover to identify the wildlife trafficker who was still running loose at the lodge.

It was a lot to take in.

I rested my elbows on the cluttered desk and massaged my temples, trying to make sense of it all. At least Twilla's weird behavior finally made sense—her unexplained absences, her sneaking around, even how she ID'ed the blood on the owl talons.

Looking back, I wondered why the idea of Ollie trapping owls for sale on the black market hadn't crossed my mind sooner. It seemed so obvious now. Maybe it was because I'd never imagined he was capable of something as despicable as wildlife trafficking. The nature photographers I knew were conservationists, not poachers. Ollie must have really needed the cash.

Come to think of it, hadn't Mason mentioned something about Ollie's income taking a hit? He'd probably turned to wildlife trafficking to make up for lost earnings. It was sad, really. The guy dedicated his entire life to documenting nature, only to end up exploiting the same creatures he celebrated with his lens.

Mason immediately sprang to mind as a prime candidate for Ollie's trafficking partner. It made sense. Their shared history and expertise would have given them extensive knowledge of animal behavior. Who would be more effective at trapping wildlife than people who spent their lives observing and capturing images of these creatures in the wild?

Although Ollie and Mason were at loggerheads, their differences seemed to revolve around Mason's dodgy editing techniques. Even if Ollie genuinely disapproved of Mason's professional ethics, it didn't rule out the possibility they were working together as traffickers, right?

Actually, their whole disagreement could have been a clever ploy to throw people off the scent. For all I knew, Ollie's public outbursts against Mason were just a smokescreen to hide their criminal partnership.

If Mason wasn't Ollie's trafficking partner, I was back at square one, and Childress had made it clear that we were running out of time. Ollie's mystery partner could skip town any day now, vanishing without a trace. The pressure was on to pinpoint Ollie's accomplice in the trafficking ring, but tracking him down was going to be way more challenging than it sounded.

Sam entered the office, carrying a takeout cup in each hand. "I thought I'd spare you my terrible coffee and pick up some hot chocolates from the cafe," he said, setting one of the cups down in front of me.

As I sipped hot chocolate, I noticed Sam eyeing me from across the desk, obviously curious about what had gone down in his office. I racked my brain for something harmless to tell him, some tidbit of information I could share without breaking my promise to Childress.

I was about to concoct a story involving Twilla and an unpaid speeding ticket when Sam raised his hand to stop me. "Don't bother. Childress was pretty specific when she asked to use my office," he said. "She told me from the get-go that I couldn't ask what you guys talked about."

"You must have a ton of questions," I acknowledged, relieved that I didn't have to make up a story for him. "I'll tell you everything just as soon as I can. For now, just take my word that everyone is safe, and everything is under control."

Admittedly, I was probably being a little optimistic about the last part, about everything being under control.

"In fact," I continued gently, "it's probably best if you pretend you never saw Twilla." I told him that Twilla had suddenly disappeared yesterday, and no one at the lodge knew where she went. For reasons I couldn't get into right now, it was important for people to think she was still missing.

"My lips are sealed," he assured me."I didn't see anything, and as far as I know, Twilla's living in a condo in Timbuktu with Elvis and JFK."

I gave his arm a gentle squeeze. "I really appreciate this, Sam. It means a lot to me that you're on board with this."

"Is there anything you can tell me?" he asked. "Any new clues about Ollie's murder?"

While I had to keep quiet about Ollie's side gig as a wildlife trafficker, I figured it wouldn't hurt to tell Sam what I'd learned about Mason.

"Well, I did a little snooping on Mason Reed earlier today," I mentioned casually.

That got Sam's attention. "You did?" he asked. "Find anything juicy?"

"I stumbled across some photography forums online. It turns out that before Ollie died, he accused Mason of doctoring some of his most popular shots. Apparently, it's common knowledge among photographers."

"Wow," he said. "I don't know much about nature photography, but that sounds like a pretty serious accusation. Makes you wonder whether Mason's as clean-cut as he appears."

"Exactly," I said, "and there's more. When I pressed Mason about where he was the night Ollie died, he got all squirrelly." I shared how Mason said he was taking night shots but had conveniently forgotten the exact location.

"Hmm," Sam said, rubbing his chin. "You know, Wanda and I might be able to dig a little deeper into this Mason situation."

Now Sam had my attention. "What exactly are you suggesting?"

"Since our lunch the other day, Wanda and I have been chatting about the case," Sam admitted. "I'm thinking we could do a little investigating on Mason. You know, see if there's anything to those photography accusations and maybe even figure out where he was the night Ollie died."

"That would be amazing," I said. "If you guys could uncover anything concrete about Mason's alibi or those doctored photos, it would be really helpful."

Sam's face broke into an excited grin. "Consider it done."

I couldn't have orchestrated it better if I'd tried. Without lifting a finger, I'd managed to recruit Sam and Wanda into my little undercover operation without breaking my promise to Childress.

"But remember," I warned him, "you and Wanda have to keep it low-key and stay safe. Nothing risky. If you find anything that seems remotely suspicious, let me know, and I'll tell Childress."

Sam gave me a playful salute. "Got it, captain." Noticing the skeptical look on my face, he added, "Don't worry, we won't do anything risky."

I glanced at my watch. Almost noon. "Yikes, I better get going. I have to get back to the lodge and grab a quick bite to eat before I relieve Fuzz at the front desk."

As we said our goodbyes, I could see the gears already turning in Sam's mind as he formulated his next steps. I had no doubt that the minute I left, he'd make a beeline to the cafe to start strategizing with Wanda.

Outside, I fired up the Birdmobile and grabbed my phone while the engine hummed to life. I quickly texted Annie to see if she'd heard anything about Big Ted's intentions to arrest Twilla.

"Lab results r in," Annie texted back. "Blood on the talons is Ollie's. Big Ted's arresting Twilla at the lodge this afternoon. (Sorry!)"

I tapped out a hasty thank-you text, promising to catch up with her later. Then I pulled away from the curb and sped back to the lodge. I had a wildlife trafficker to track down and a murder to solve.

And time was running out.

CHAPTER 20

I was seconds away from sinking my teeth into double-decker PB&J when Fuzz came charging into the kitchen, with Charley hot on his heels.

"Drop that sandwich, we got trouble," Fuzz said, wringing his hands. Charley let out a little "woof" and spun around in a circle, picking up on Fuzz's nervous energy.

I set the sandwich on a plate. "What's going on?"

"Big Ted just pulled up in that Crown Vic of his, and he's got the entire force with him. Both deputies," Fuzz exclaimed wide-eyed.

I stole a glance out the kitchen window and saw Big Ted strutting across the parking lot. His two deputies trailed behind him, tripping over themselves to keep up, like ducklings scurrying after their mother.

Fuzz turned to Charley. "You're on watch." Charley gave a little woof to acknowledge he was on it, then peered out the kitchen door like a sentinel. He shot a quick glance back at us, tail wagging energetically, as if to say he had guard duty covered.

"Okay, I'll deal with Big Ted," I sighed, casting a final, regretful glance at my untouched sandwich. "Wish me luck."

"Good luck," Fuzz said. "We'll be right here if you need us."

I found Big Ted in the lobby, adjusting his duty belt. He acknowledged me with a nod while his deputies lingered in the background.

"Afternoon, Ms. Palmer," he said, his voice taking on a deliberately formal note. "I'm sorry to say I have some bad news."

I had a pretty good idea what that bad news was.

"We have evidence that connects Twilla Jankowsky to the murder of Ollie Harlow," he announced. "I'm here to place her under arrest."

Even though I knew Big Ted was likely to arrest Twilla, I hadn't taken the time to plan my reaction. Should I pretend to be surprised? Definitely. Show defiance? Probably not a smart move. Ultimately, I decided to go with a mix of manufactured shock and a bit of genuine honesty.

"Twilla?" I echoed, expressing as much astonishment as I could muster. "I'd like to help you, Chief, but she's not here. She packed up and left yesterday, totally out of the blue. I honestly have no idea where she is now." That wasn't a complete lie. I really didn't know Twilla's current whereabouts.

Big Ted's lip twitched. This obviously wasn't the response he'd expected. "Well," he said, drawing out the word as he processed the news, "then I guess I'll have to issue an APB on her."

He narrowed his eyes like he was trying to read my thoughts. If I had to guess, I'd say he was trying to figure out whether or not I was telling him the truth. I met his look with my best poker face, determined to keep my expression as plain and convincing as possible.

Big Ted blinked first. "Alright, Ms. Palmer. I'll take your word for it, but if Twilla gets in touch with you, I expect to hear about it immediately. Got it?"

"Of course," I lied. Truth be told, Twilla had already gotten in touch with me once, and I was pretty sure she'd contact me again soon. "If she contacts me, you'll be the first to know."

Satisfied, Big Ted readjusted his belt and started to leave. Halfway to the door, he swung back around. "By the way, I saw that article in the paper today. Just so you know, I didn't say anything to that reporter about the lodge."

Fantastic. Apparently, Tyler Barnes and the Daily Herald had published their story and judging by Big Ted's tone, it didn't paint a very flattering picture of the lodge. Masking my surprise, I managed a polite smile and thanked him, then sent him on his way.

Heading back to the kitchen, I spotted Fred Caruso at a table, a cup of something hot in hand and a small mountain of cookies in front of him. He motioned me over.

When I reached his table, I asked if everything was okay. He assured me that everything was fine, and Lois was taking her afternoon nap. Then he casually mentioned they planned to check out tomorrow.

"We've seen all the owls we could hope to see," he said with a chuckle. "We're all 'owled out,' as Lois says."

I mentioned that owl sightings were getting scarce and several other guests were also planning to leave soon. "But it's been wonderful having you stay with us," I told him. Fred smiled warmly, expressing his appreciation in return.

As I turned to leave, my eyes landed on the newspaper sitting on the table. "Mind if I borrow your paper?"

"It's yours, my dear," Fred said, handing it to me. "I don't believe a word of what they said about the lodge. Some of these reporters . . ." He trailed off with a dismissive wave.

As I walked away, I thumbed through the newspaper until I came across Tyler's article on page two. It wasn't on the front page, which was a minor miracle, but that didn't soften the blow of the headline: "Prominent Photographer's Death Now a Murder Investigation."

The article went on to describe the grim details of Ollie's death, and how Beechtree PD has officially ruled the case a homicide. Tyler mentioned Loon Lodge several times and noted that a person of interest in the case had close ties to the lodge. He even dragged last summer's incident with the mayor into it, implying that the lodge played a role in her death. The article ended with a jab at me, saying, "Loon Lodge's proprietor, Honey Palmer, declined to comment."

His insinuations about "close ties to the lodge" were infuriatingly vague yet damaging. He made it sound like the lodge was some sort of criminal headquarters. Declined to comment? The next time I ran into Tyler Barnes, I'd have plenty to say.

In the kitchen, Fuzz was sitting on a stool at the counter, polishing a set of old brass doorknobs we'd been meaning to repurpose. Charley remained posted by the door on guard duty.

"So, what did he want?" Fuzz asked.

I filled him in on Big Ted's visit and his intention to arrest Twilla for Ollie's murder. Fuzz shook his head, a smile on his lips. "Classic Big Ted, always a mile off the mark," he said and went back to polishing his doorknob.

Changing the subject, I asked Fuzz if he'd seen the article in the paper. "Yeah, I saw it," he admitted sheepishly. "I didn't tell you about it because I didn't want to add to your worries. These things tend to blow over."

"I'm not sure it's so simple this time," I said. "We have to find out who killed Ollie and set the record straight about the lodge." We were also running out of time to track down

Ollie's trafficking partner before they left Beechtree, but I kept that part to myself.

"Have you seen Evie around?" I asked.

He nodded. "Yeah, she stopped by. Said she had to run out to get some supplies for tomorrow's breakfast bar."

I took a second to think about how I wanted to ask my next question. "So, Evie mentioned you popped the question. What the heck were you thinking, Fuzz?"

"I want to marry her, that's what I was thinking," he said as he set down the doorknob. "And believe me, it's not because I feel like I have to. I genuinely love the woman, but she just doesn't seem to appreciate how serious I am."

"Well, I wouldn't be so sure that she doesn't understand how serious you are. Maybe it's something else." I didn't want to betray Evie's confidence, so I kept it vague. "You know, she's been married a couple of times before and those relationships didn't end very well."

Fuzz's expression mellowed. "I've been thinking about that," he admitted, his voice tinged with a hint of defeat. "But what's it gonna take to prove to her that I'm different, that we're different? Maybe I need to give it more time. She might just need a bit longer to realize what we have is the real deal, not like those other times."

I offered a half-smile. "We're quite the pair, huh? Both of us stuck in neutral and not sure how to move forward."

"You've got that right," he replied. We sat quietly for a few minutes, each of us lost in our own thoughts and worries. Suddenly, he sprang up from his recliner. "Grab your coat," he announced.

"Why? Where are we going?"

Fuzz was halfway to the door when he whistled for Charley, who bounded over with his tail wagging. "There's someplace we need to be," he said.

I followed him to his pickup truck, parked behind the

lodge. As we pulled out of the parking lot, we passed Evie on her way back from the supply run. I shot her a wave and sent her a text, asking her to cover the front desk while Fuzz and I ran an errand.

Even though I had no idea what the errand might be.

CHAPTER 21

Fuzz slowed the pickup to a crawl as we rolled past the owl blind. A couple of cars were parked haphazardly in the little parking area, and I could see a handful of owl watchers huddled together inside the blind—stragglers hoping to catch a glimpse of a snowy owl before they were left for good.

Further on, we turned onto a driveway that I would have completely missed if it weren't for faint tire tracks in the snow marking its entrance. The truck bounced up and down as we jolted along the uneven path, branches scraping the side panels.

"The driveway could use a little plowing," Fuzz remarked, downshifting to push through the deeper drifts.

We continued on past the point any normal driveway would have ended, winding deeper into the snowy forest. It dawned on me that this wasn't a driveway at all. It was an old access road dating back to the days when Hayes Landing was a functioning airport.

As we rounded a curve, an enormous hangar appeared, its corrugated metal streaked with rust. The instant I saw the building, I was transported back to mornings spent watching Piper Cubs and Cessnas gracefully descend to the runway and the scent of hot pancakes drenched in maple syrup drifting through the air.

Every year, Fuzz and Mom would bring me to Hayes Landing for the annual fly-in breakfast fundraiser. We'd stuff ourselves with pancakes at the long tables inside the hangar, then wander outside to watch the planes take off, propellers blurring as they gathered speed. The place seemed magical when I was a kid.

Now? Not so much.

Continuing past the hangar, Fuzz brought the pickup to a stop outside a rundown two-story house and turned off the engine. The house's clapboard siding had faded to gray, and its missing shingles and boarded up windows gave it an abandoned appearance. Yet, a snow shovel propped by the front door and the tire tracks in the snow suggested that someone still lived here.

"Wildcat Hayes?" I asked.

Fuzz nodded, a smile breaking through his beard. "Yep, this is her roost."

We had barely stepped out of the truck when the front door burst open, and a figure appeared in the doorway. It was Wildcat. She was wearing her trademark blaze orange beanie and hunting vest, along with a worn-out sweater, flannel pajama bottoms and muck boots, and she casually cradled an ancient hinge-action shotgun in her arms.

Before either of us could react, a streak of black and white fur darted out from behind Wildcat. Charley charged forward to confront the creature, and I braced for a violent clash. Instead, they tumbled together in a frenzy of fur and began wrestling playfully in the snow. Tail wagging, Charley seemed overjoyed to see his old friend, who I now realized was a French bulldog.

"Fuzz Stillman, you old so-and-so! Get on up here and give me a proper hello!" Wildcat called out, her grim expression melting into a welcoming grin. "Looks like Charley and Frenchie are picking up where they left off. How long's it been since they've seen each other?"

"Oh, it's been a while," Fuzz said, watching the dogs romp. "I think the last time I was out this way was when I bought that old welder from you last year."

"That sounds about right." Wildcat held the door open. "Well come on in, you two. Don't stand around jawin' all day in this cold."

I stomped the snow from my boots and stepped inside. The house's interior appeared just as ramshackle as its exterior with peeling wallpaper, threadbare furniture, and worn wooden floors that slanted at odd angles.

Aviation memorabilia covered every surface—framed photos of Wildcat posing with vintage planes on the walls, model aircraft hanging from the ceiling, shelves crammed with books on aerodynamics and flight. On the mantle, there was a faded photo of a young Wildcat in her flight suit, standing beside a handsome dark-haired man I assumed was her late husband.

Peering through the living room window, I could see the owl blind in the distance. A spotting scope was mounted on a tripod in front of the window, presumably so Wildcat could monitor the old airfield. I hoped she'd used it to keep an eye on things at the owl blind too.

"Make yourselves at home," she said, shuffling into the small kitchen. The dogs moved to a corner of the room and began a spirited tug-of-war with an old rope.

I made myself comfortable on the lumpy couch, while Fuzz claimed the armchair. "What brings you guys out here?" Wildcat asked, her voice echoing from the kitchen where she busied herself making tea.

"Well, Honey here is looking into that photographer fellow's murder," Fuzz said, "and I thought you might have some information, seeing how they found him at the owl blind and all."

From the kitchen, Wildcat shared her regrets about having to sell the airfield. She admitted she hadn't saved enough money for retirement, any money really, and the runway needed so much work—way more than she could afford. The decision to sell was tough, but she took some comfort in knowing that the land was now in the hands of the land trust.

Her tone brightened when she mentioned how much fun she'd had watching the owls—and the owl watchers—these last few weeks. "It's been a hoot," she said.

I cleared my throat. "So, Wildcat, we know Ollie Harlow was found at the owl blind. Did you happen to notice anything unusual that might give us a clue about who killed him?"

Wildcat shuffled back in, handing us cups of tea on chipped saucers. "I always liked that photographer fella's pictures." She settled into her recliner with a groan. "He used to take pictures of airplanes too. Did you know that?"

"No, I didn't," I said. "Anyway, did the police talk to you?"

She guffawed. "Talk to me? Hah! If you could call it that. Big Ted showed up the day they found the photographer's body and asked me if I'd seen anything strange. I told him I was worshipping the porcelain god all night thanks to some bad mayo. So nope, didn't see a darn thing."

Wildcat paused to take a big slurp of tea. "Just between us, Big Ted couldn't wait to get out of here. He's always been a little skittish around me."

"Can't imagine why," Fuzz chuckled.

I let out an exasperated sigh. "Shoot. I was hoping you might've seen something that could help us."

Wildcat's eyes lit up. "I never said I didn't see anything. Just that I hadn't seen anything odd that particular night, on account of my mayo troubles. Big Ted didn't ask me about any other times, so that's all I told him."

"You mean you really did see some strange things? Like what?"

"Those owl watchers are a wacky crew!" she said and launched into a series of colorful stories about the quirky things the birdwatchers had been up to at the owl blind. With each story, her descriptions got more animated and the scenarios more absurd. By the end, we were all laughing hysterically.

After we caught our breath, I guided the conversation back to the matter at hand. "Did you notice Ollie around the owl blind often?"

Wildcat nodded, refilling our mugs from a porcelain teapot. "Sure did. In fact, I saw that beat up old van of his parked near the owl blind plenty of nights. It was the only vehicle left in the lot when the police came for his body, so I figured it had to be his."

"But that wasn't the only vehicle I saw," she continued. "There was usually another van there too, seemed like a newer model from what I could tell."

"Wildcat, any chance you got a good enough look at that other van to provide a better description?" I asked.

She narrowed her eyes, concentrating as she tried to recall the details of the other van. "Well let's see . . . it was definitely newer than Ollie's rusted out old clunker. I'd say no more than a few years old. It was white, maybe with some blue detailing. Had one of those pop-up sleeper tops, so I'm guessing it could double as a pretty comfy little camper."

As she spoke, an uneasy feeling washed over me. Her description of the van sounded alarmingly similar to the Carusos' camper.

The Carusos looked like such a sweet old couple, but what if they weren't as harmless as they appeared? Ollie had been involved in some shady stuff. Were the Carusos involved in that too? Late-night meet-ups at the owl blind didn't seem very innocent.

Mention of the pop-up sleeper top launched Fuzz and Wildcat into a debate over the merits of various types of RVs. I tuned most of it out—my mind was still reeling with questions about what Ollie and the Carusos could have been up to out here under the cover of darkness.

I waited for a lull in the RV conversation before asking my next question. "This is probably a long shot, but any chance you happened to notice if that other camper van was at the owl blind the night Ollie was killed?"

Wildcat shook her head apologetically. "Sorry hon, can't say for sure. That bad mayonnaise really did a number on me. I was in the bathroom so much I didn't have much time to keep an eye on the parking lot. Anything's possible I suppose. But like I said, I saw those two camper vans parked there almost every night. Hard to say what they were up to since there's just that one little lamppost in the lot, but they were definitely there."

"Well, I appreciate you taking the time to chat with us," Fuzz said, rising from the faded floral armchair. "It's been a pleasure as always, Wildcat."

"Likewise, Fuzz," Wildcat replied warmly. She followed us to the front door. "And don't you worry about that nonsense article in the paper. Bunch of muckrakers if you ask me. You know I've got your back if you need me."

"Right back at you, Wildcat," Fuzz said.

The dogs emerged from behind the couch. Charley seemed reluctant to leave his old friend Frenchie behind, but with some encouragement, we managed to peel him away and load him into Fuzz's pickup truck.

As we drove back down the access road, I looked out over the abandoned airfield. I could just make out the owl blind parking area in the distance, and I imagined Ollie's van parked there night after night. What had he been doing out here? And what did it have to do with the Carusos?

Fuzz interrupted my thoughts. "That other camper van Wildcat described sure sounded a lot like the Carusos' van, didn't it?"

"Yeah, it definitely fits her description," I agreed. "Late night meetings between Ollie and the Carusos? Maybe it's time to take a closer look at that sweet old couple."

Fuzz agreed. "Might be worth finding out what they were up to out here too."

"You and Wildcat seemed pretty chummy back there. Tell me again, how do you two know each other?"

Fuzz laughed, keeping his eyes on the road. "Well, if you must know, Wildcat and I dated for a short spell back in high school. Long before I met your mother, of course."

My eyebrows shot up. Somehow I couldn't picture a young Fuzz and Wildcat as a couple.

He continued, "Yeah, we were a pair of aces, that's for sure. Wildcat was the daredevil, always zipping around on that little motorbike of hers. I could barely keep up with her. We had some good times, but in the end we decided we made better friends than sweethearts. We've been on friendly terms ever since."

"I can totally picture it—you and Wildcat showing up to prom in a powder blue tux and a fancy dress. That must have been quite the sight."

Fuzz grinned, "Oh, it was."

CHAPTER 22

The late afternoon sun slanted through the tall pines as Fuzz's old truck rattled up the lodge's driveway. Through the lobby window, I saw Evie seated at the front desk.

"Thanks for the adventure," I said, hopping out. "You coming in?"

Fuzz looked over at Evie and stroked his beard. "I think Charley and me are gonna call it a day. See you tomorrow, kiddo."

I watched his pickup lumber back down the driveway toward his cabin, then I headed into the lodge where I found Evie once again engrossed in her paperback.

"Hey there, stranger," she said, peering up from her book. "What have you been up to?"

It took every bit of willpower I had not to divulge what I'd learned from Childress, especially the bombshell about Ollie's secret life as a wildlife trafficker. I would have loved having Evie on board to help me track down Ollie's partner, but a promise was a promise.

"Fuzz and I just got back from Wildcat's place, over at Hayes Landing."

"How'd you end up at Wildcat's?" she asked, closing her book.

"It was Fuzz's idea actually," I explained. "I guess the two of them go way back. Did you know they were high school sweethearts?"

Evie tried to play it cool, but it was clear she was hearing about Fuzz and Wildcat's fifty-year-old romance for the first time. A flicker of jealousy crossed her face before she got a hold of herself.

"Did you find out anything worthwhile from your little visit?" she asked, a slight edge in her voice.

"We did, actually," I replied. "I'm still trying to piece it all together, but I'll fill you in on the details over dinner."

"Speaking of dinner, what are you in the mood for?"

"To be totally honest, I don't have many options at the cabin," I said. "Some expired yogurt and a couple cans of soup."

"That settles it. We're going to the Hop House." She flopped the closed sign on the front desk and turned off the lights. "I've been jonesing for pizza anyway."

Half an hour later, Evie and I were settled at a table close to the Hop House's wood-fired pizza oven. The place was buzzing with early diners, and the bar was standing room only. The sound of John Mellencamp's "Small Town" drifted from the jukebox, adding to the laid-back vibe.

A young waitress, her face dotted with freckles, hurried over with menus in hand. Not that we needed them. Since Evie was still recovering from girls' night, we'd already decided to skip IPAs in favor of tall glasses of Hop House root beer. As for the pizzas, I went straight for the Hawaiian, while Evie opted for a mushroom with double cheese.

After the freckly waitress left to put in our orders, Evie asked how things were going with Sam.

"I called him before we left the lodge. He's chasing down a hot lead on Mason Reed with Wanda."

"Leave it to those two to go all in, right?" She laughed. Then, out of the blue, she asked, "So, how's Fuzz? Did he say anything about me today?"

It was clear that her issues with Fuzz were taking a toll on her, but I still didn't want to get caught in the middle of it. Rather than diving into the details of what I'd talked about with Fuzz, I decided to take a more subtle approach.

"I think he really misses you," I said, "And it's pretty obvious that you miss him too. It just seems like you're having a communication problem."

"Communication problem? Oh, I think there's a little more to it than that," she replied. "Listen, Honey, I never got to meet your mom, but everyone says she was one of a kind/"

"She was. I miss her every single day."

"That's my point," she continued. "Of course Fuzz wants to get married again—he had such a great run the first time. Me? I'm a three-time loser. What if I'm just not cut out for marriage? I mean, your mom set a pretty high bar."

I hadn't thought about it that way. No wonder Evie was resisting the idea of marrying Fuzz. She didn't see herself as marriage material.

"I get it. Mom was amazing, but don't be too hard on yourself. You're amazing too, you know. What if it works out this time? It'd be a shame to miss out on something great just because you're too scared to give it another shot."

Before she could respond, the front door swung open and Maddie strolled in. When she spotted us, I waved her over, and she pulled up a chair.

"What brings you here?" I asked.

"I just finished my shift at the ranger station and

promised Liliana I'd stop by," she said, then explained, "Liliana's working tonight."

Right on cue, Liliana popped out from behind the bar and dashed to our table, setting an IPA in front of Maddie and two root beers for Evie and me.

"What's the occasion? Did someone forget to send me an invite for the party?" Liliana joked, claiming the empty chair.

"No occasion. Evie and I were just craving pizza. In fact, I was just about to share some Ollie news with her and Maddie."

"Don't let me stop you," Liliana said, scanning the room. "This place can take manage itself for a while. Spill the tea!"

"Well, Fuzz and I were talking about Ollie this afternoon, and on a whim, we decided to swing by Wildcat Hayes's place." For Evie's benefit, I skipped over the part about Fuzz and Wildcat being old flames.

I explained that from her living room, Wildcat had a clear view of the owl blind and the parking area. Unfortunately, she didn't see anything the night of the murder. "She was stuck in the bathroom most of the night. Bad mayo," I added, eliciting a wince from Evie.

"The silver lining is that there's a pole light in the parking area and Wildcat's kept an eye on comings and goings at the owl blind," I continued. "According to her, she's noticed Ollie's van parked there a lot, usually late at night."

"Okay, but so what?" Evie interjected. "We all know these photography types can be obsessive about night shots. So it makes sense that his van would be in the parking area at all hours, right?"

"Yes, but here's the kicker. Ollie's van was never parked there alone. There was always another vehicle that arrived and left the parking area at similar times. And Wildcat's description of that vehicle is a dead ringer for the Carusos' camper van."

BELL BECK

Liliana's eyes bulged out of their sockets. "The Carusos? That adorable elderly couple staying at the lodge?"

"I can't picture them involved in something like this," Evie protested. "They're the sweetest people on the planet."

"Regardless, their van was in that parking area next to Ollie's van, late at night, on a regular basis. And I highly doubt they were there snapping night photos. Have you ever noticed them with any photography equipment, Evie?"

Evie shook her head. "Never. In fact, Lois mentioned that photography wasn't their thing. Too much gear to lug around. They preferred birdwatching with binoculars."

I mentioned that the Carusos were creatures of habit. They'd head out early in the morning for birdwatching and return late in the afternoon. Once they were back at the lodge, they tended to stay in for the evening, as far as I could tell.

Maddie jogged my memory about something I'd brought up at girls' night about the Carusos being night owls. I clarified that it was more about their sleep troubles than anything else. Fred battled insomnia and relied on sleeping pills to catch some Zs. As for Lois, well, she often spent a good part of the night curled up with a book by the fire.

The aroma of hot pizza filled the air as the waitress arrived with our order. She placed the steaming pies in front of Evie and me, along with extra plates. Everyone grabbed a slice and dug in, even Liliana, who said that it was shaping up be a hectic night at the Hop House and this might be her last chance to eat for a while.

I was halfway through my second slice when a thought occurred to me. "Oh my gosh!" I blurted out. "I just remembered something. A few days ago, Fred told me he'd picked up a new pair of night vision binoculars, and he was all excited about trying them out that night."

"Wait a minute," Liliana said. "Are we suggesting the

Carusos have been leading some kind of secret life after dark?"

Maddie nodded slowly. "At the very least, we know that one or both of them were meeting up with Ollie at the owl blind after dark."

"My money's on Fred. He's the one with the night vision binoculars. And Lois seems too frail to be sneaking around at night," I said, taking another bite of Hawaiian.

"No argument there, but it still doesn't make sense," Evie replied. "What were Fred and Ollie doing out there?"

Unfortunately, I had a pretty good idea what Fred and Ollie were doing at the most popular owl hotspot in the county under the cover of darkness. Trapping owls and then selling them on the black market.

And it was looking more and more like it might have gotten Ollie killed.

After we finished our pizzas, Liliana returned to work, and Maddie headed home to her cabin. "I'm totally wiped," she sighed. "I can't wait to ditch this uniform, slip into my PJs, and binge-watch 'Only Murders in the Building.'"

With Maddie gone, Evie and I stuck around the Hop House for a bit, shooting the breeze. When the conversation veered toward the topic of Ollie and Fred, I casually steered it back to small talk. Under normal circumstances, I'd have loved to swap murder theories with Evie, but my current circumstances were anything but normal. Any talk about Ollie and Fred would have forced me to either bend the truth or straight up lie to my best friend about why the pair had been meeting up at Hayes Landing, and I didn't want to do that.

Instead, we talked about when we expected to see the first red-winged blackbirds of the season and the latest books we'd read and how much we both hated TikTok. The natural rhythm of our conversation felt nice, like things were back to normal and we were just a couple of friends sharing the dream of running a mountain lodge together. For a few minutes, I even managed to forget that there was a crazed killer on the loose at the lodge.

Before long, we spotted a group of older birders a few tables over, downing drafts, all smiles and laughter. They recognized us from the lodge and waved us over. It took a little persuading, but eventually they cajoled us into joining their circle. Evie and I ended up sticking around for a drink, exchanging stories about our birding adventures.

When we finally returned to my cabin, I immediately changed into my pajamas and rushed through my nighttime routine. As I brushed my teeth, it dawned on me that I'd meant to call Childress earlier to share the news about Ollie's van and my suspicions regarding Fred's involvement in the trafficking ring, and possibly even Ollie's murder. A quick check of the tiny clock by the sink confirmed it was too late now. "First thing in the morning," I promised myself.

Climbing into bed, I skipped my usual habit of reading a few chapters on my Kindle. Tomorrow was shaping up to be a big day. I'd call Childress, then she would apprehend Fred and clear the lodge's good name.

And Tyler Barnes would have to print a big, fat retraction in the Daily Herald.

CHAPTER 23

A jingling sound jolted me awake, and I squinted at the glare of the alarm clock. 2:37 a.m. Groaning, I groped around in the darkness for my phone, accidentally knocking over the glass of water I kept on the nightstand. Still half-asleep, I raised the phone to my ear.

"Honey! Oh, thank goodness you answered," Lois's voice crackled through the phone, a sense of urgency in her tone.

"What's going on?" I blurted out, sitting up straight in bed.

"It's Fred. He won't wake up. I think he might have had a heart attack or something. He's not responding!" Her words dissolved into tears.

I leaped out of bed, clutching the phone to my ear as I pulled on my jeans. "Take a deep breath, Lois. I'm on my way. Did you call 911?"

"N-no, I haven't," she stammered. "I just ran to the front desk to find your number. Please hurry!"

"I'll be right there. Try to stay calm." I ended the call and shoved my feet into boots, a mixture of adrenaline and dread coursing through me.

Outside, the moon cast an eerie glow over the snow as I

dashed along the path toward the lodge. My fingers trembled as I dialed 911 and relayed the situation to the dispatcher.

After hanging up with 911, it hit me that I'd ran out of the cabin without filling Evie in on what was going on. I dialed her number from speed dial, and she picked up after a couple of rings. Speaking rapidly, I urged her to get to the lodge as quickly as possible—there was something wrong with Fred.

As soon as I entered the lodge, Lois met me, her face streaked with tears. "He's upstairs," she managed through her sobs, fresh tears welling up in her eyes. "I just . . . I can't bear to see him like that again," she faltered.

"Don't worry, just stay here," I reassured her before heading upstairs to their room.

The room was dimly lit, with only a hint of moonlight seeping through the curtains. I approached Fred's side of the bed and flicked on the bedside lamp. Even in the faint light, his skin looked unnaturally pale and waxy. I searched for any signs of life. No pulse, no breath. It didn't take a medical degree to tell that Fred was gone.

The room seemed to be in order. While Fred lay neatly tucked in on his side of the bed, Lois's side remained untouched. Not a single crease marred the smooth bedspread. Their suitcases stood stacked by the door, zipped shut.

If it weren't for the lifeless body on the mattress, I could have easily mistaken it for a room ready and waiting for its next occupants.

Evie waited for me in the hallway. I gave her a small shake of my head, and her face fell.

"Oh boy," she whispered.

"I'm pretty sure he's passed," I said softly. "If it's any comfort, it looks like he went peacefully."

Evie sprang into action. "I'll stay with Lois in the great

room. Fuzz and Charley are outside waiting for the EMTs, and Maddie's on her way."

As I watched her hustle down the stairs, I pulled out my phone to dial Childress, mentally berating myself for not doing it the night before. With Fred's ties to Ollie's trafficking operation seeming more and more likely, I couldn't help but wonder if reaching out sooner might have changed things. Now, we might never definitively connect Fred to Ollie and the trafficking ring.

Childress picked up after a few rings, her voice sounding groggy. "

Sorry to call like this," I started, "but there's a situation at the lodge. One of our guests seems to have passed away in his sleep."

"Natural causes?" she asked, suddenly sounding wide awake.

"Probably, but it's a bit more complicated than that. We might have lost our best lead," I explained.

"Got it. I'm on my way. Keep the room off-limits to everyone except the EMTs until I get there," she instructed, ending the call.

Slipping my phone into my back pocket, I returned to the lobby just in time to witness the EMTs rushing in with Maddie following closely behind. Fuzz trailed in afterward, with a serious case of bed head.

"Where to?" asked one of the EMTs, a slender woman with short blonde hair.

Maddie motioned toward the stairs, leading the way. Meanwhile, Fuzz paused to corral Charley, who seemed eager to join the commotion, gently holding him back by his collar.

"Come on, buddy, let's go brew some coffee," he murmured to Charley, guiding him to the kitchen. Charley shot me a puzzled glance, confused about why he couldn't be involved in the unfolding drama.

I found Evie and Lois in the great room, huddled by the fire with a blanket draped over Lois' shoulders. Evie suggested making some tea, which Lois gratefully accepted.

As Evie disappeared into the kitchen to brew the tea, I settled down next to Lois on the sofa. Taking a deep breath, I asked her to walk me through the events of the past few hours, explaining that any details she could provide might be helpful for the EMTs.

With a shaky voice, Lois recounted that she and Fred had packed their bags to leave in the morning. Around eleven o'clock, Fred had taken a sleeping pill, and she had made him a hot toddy to help him sleep. She spent the rest of her evening reading by the fire in the great room, only discovering Fred's condition when she went upstairs a few minutes before she called me.

Evie returned with Lois' tea just as several guests began trickling downstairs in robes and slippers, whispering questions about the ambulance outside. I did my best to reassure them that everything was under control, explaining that another guest was experiencing a medical issue, and gently directing them back upstairs.

After what felt like an eternity, Maddie descended the stairs with a solemn expression. She motioned for Evie and me to join her. "He's gone," she said simply. Together, the three of us returned to the sofa to break the news to Lois.

Lois took the news better than expected. She didn't scream or cry out, not even when the EMTs carried Fred's covered body down the stairs on a stretcher. Instead, a quiet sadness seemed to envelop her, like a heavy blanket.

When Fuzz and Charley emerged from the kitchen, carrying a tray of coffee and looking a bit bewildered, Evie suggested they escort Lois back to their cabin. "Great idea," Fuzz quickly agreed. Together, the trio headed towards the door, leaving Maddie and me alone near the fire.

"What did the EMTs say?" I asked.

Maddie shook her head. "Not much. They're leaning toward natural causes, but we won't know for sure until the ME examines the body."

Out of nowhere, Childress materialized beside us. "Fuzz mentioned I could find you here. What's the latest?" Her gaze shifted between Maddie and me.

I quickly briefed her on the recent events: Lois's frantic call, discovering Fred lifeless in his bed, and the EMTs' preliminary conclusion of natural causes.

Childress took the information in stride, her cool demeanor unshaken. "Well, I've already dealt with Big Ted, so he won't be causing any trouble," she stated, then turned her attention to me. "Can we chat privately?"

Maddie shot Childress a skeptical glance. "I'll be in my cabin if you need me," she announced, striding across the great room toward the door.

"Alright, spill it. How did you manage to get Big Ted off our backs? I'm dying to know."

Childress explained that under normal circumstances, the state police would have intervened as soon as Ollie's death was ruled a homicide. However, they were already investigating Ollie for wildlife trafficking. Rather than risking tipping off Ollie's associates, they decided to let Big Ted stumble around for a while."

I couldn't help but chuckle at the thought of Big Ted unwittingly running interference for the state police all this time. Although it had been painful to watch, I had to appreciate the cleverness of their strategy.

"After this latest death," Childress continued, "I convinced Big Ted that it would be best for everyone if we took the lead on the investigation. He wasn't thrilled about it, but he agreed to step aside."

Then Childress changed the subject and asked if I had uncovered any information about Ollie's accomplice.

"Believe it or not, I think I've figured out who Ollie was working with, but you're not going to like it," I said.

She arched an eyebrow. "Don't tell me it's the dead guy."

"The dead guy is Fred Caruso, and I'm pretty sure he was in cahoots with Ollie," I revealed.

She looked stunned. "Fred Caruso? The old guy from Cincinnati?"

"That's him," I confirmed. "I didn't want to believe it myself, but Wildcat Hayes spotted Fred's van parked at the owl blind after hours on several occasions. Right next to Ollie's van." I also mentioned Fred's boasting about his high-end night vision binoculars. Additionally, I pointed out that Lois seemed too frail to be directly involved. She might have known about it, but I felt confident she didn't participate in trapping or selling owls.

"Alright, here's the million dollar question," Childress said. "How certain are you that our guy died of natural causes?"

I told her the EMTs suspected it was natural causes, but the medical examiner would have to make the final call. Until then, it was impossible to know how Fred had died.

Childress shot me one of her looks. "I wouldn't be so sure about that."

CHAPTER 24

The idea of snooping around a dead man's room felt pretty shady. But Childress had just suggested we dig through Fred's belongings to piece together how he died and was already heading up the stairs. With a sigh, I trailed after her.

As we walked down the hallway, old floorboards groaned beneath our feet. Reaching the Carusos' room, Childress quietly turned the knob, and we entered, softly closing the door behind us.

I flipped the light switch, blinking against the sudden brightness. The room looked the same as before: tidy and organized, with a few personal items neatly arranged on the oak dresser. Last time I was here, it was for a medical call—this visit felt a little creepy.

Childress, on the other hand, seemed unfazed at all by the fact that someone had just died here and went straight to Fred's nightstand to sift through its contents. I hovered awkwardly as she methodically picked through personal effects like magazines, tissues, and reading glasses.

"Go ahead and look around," she suggested without

looking up. I nodded silently and drifted to Lois's side of the bed, aimlessly poking through her few possessions.

There wasn't a whole lot to poke through—just a worn-out romance novel, another set of reading glasses, and a small bottle of hand lotion. I grabbed the book and casually flipped through its pages. It was standard romance fare, featuring a bare-chested hunk embracing a swooning lady on the cover.

Childress moved away from the nightstand and asked me to go over Lois' version of events before she found her husband dead.

"Lois told me that she and Fred were busy packing that evening," I explained. "At some point, she made him a hot toddy, and after taking a sleeping pill, he went to sleep. Lois spent some time reading by the fire downstairs. When she returned to their room, Fred was unresponsive. That's when she ran to the lobby to call me."

"Alright, let's have a look in the bathroom," she suggested, walking briskly through the room.

Right away, my eyes landed on Fred's shaving kit, right next to Lois's makeup bag on the counter. As Childress peered behind the shower curtain, I took a look inside the shaving kit. Razor, shaving cream, toothpaste—all the usual stuff. Lois's makeup bag was just as ordinary, filled with an assortment of creams and beauty products.

"Huh, that's odd," I mumbled to myself.

"What's odd?" she asked, pulling the shower curtain shut with a snap.

"Fred's sleeping pills are gone. They're not here, and I didn't notice them in the bedroom either. Did you?"

"Nope, I haven't seen them. Maybe he threw them out." She looked inside the bathroom bin before heading to the bedroom to check the trash there. Still nothing.

"Fred just got that prescription refilled," I pointed out. "That bottle should have been almost full."

Childress shrugged. "Well, we're done here." She retrieved a small container of hand sanitizer from her pocket and gave us each a squirt.

"What's next?" I asked.

"Now it's time to have a chat with the widow Caruso."

When we arrived at Fuzz and Evie's cabin, I found Fuzz lounging in his recliner, feet propped up, while Evie comforted Lois on the couch. Charley was stretched out on a braided rug in front of the fire, snoring like a freight train.

Lois appeared more put together than I expected her to be, though it was obvious she'd been crying. I introduced her to Childress, who expressed her sympathy and then mentioned she needed to ask Lois some questions about Fred.

Lois nodded courageously. "Of course, anything to help."

Fuzz saw his chance to slip away. "I should go de-ice the walkways before someone breaks a hip," he said. He whistled for Charley, "Come on, boy, let's let these ladies have some privacy."

"I'm gonna head out too," Evie chimed in, standing up. She shot Lois a supportive smile. "I'll get the breakfast bar started. I'm sure everyone's going to be hungry."

Donning their winter gear, Fuzz and Evie headed out with Charley trotting behind them, leaving the three of us sitting by the fire.

"I know this is difficult, but can you walk me through what happened before you found your husband?" Childress asked. "Even the smallest details can make a difference."

Lois took a shaky breath. "Last night Fred and I were

upstairs, packing our things. We were planning to check out today. Around ten, I made him a hot toddy to help him relax. He took his usual sleeping pill and went to bed by eleven. I wasn't sleepy yet, so I headed down to the great room to read by the fire for a while. It's what I do when I can't doze off."

She paused, wiping her eyes with a tissue. "When I went back upstairs around two-thirty, I could tell something was wrong. Fred was just lying there, not looking right. I rushed over and shook him, but he didn't respond. That's when I called Honey for help."

"The EMTs didn't tell me anything. Do they have any idea what happened?" Lois asked, a look of desperation in her eyes. "Was it a heart attack?"

Childress scribbled a few notes on her pad. "We'll have to wait for the medical examiner to determine the cause of death. Did your husband have a history of heart problems?"

"Oh, he had his fair share of issues, but Fred was never one to admit to any of them," Lois said. "We both had our health struggles. Comes with the territory at our age, I guess."

Childress nodded sympathetically. "I get it. Some nights, I toss and turn for hours before I nod off." Leaning closer, she added, "It sounds like you and Fred both dealt with insomnia too. I imagine those sleeping pills were a lifesaver."

Her seamless transition from complaining about aging to casually mentioning sleeping pills was seriously impressive. No wonder Big Ted felt intimidated by her. Childress didn't mess around.

"The pills were a lifesaver for Fred," Lois clarified. "The poor man struggled to sleep through the night without them. Me? I've always preferred a nice cup of chamomile tea and a good book."

Lois flashed me a tired smile. "Honey has been so considerate, setting out tea for me every night so I can read by the fire until the early hours. I'll take that over medication any day."

Then, out of nowhere, Childress' tone changed, and she threw a curveball into the conversation. "Mrs. Caruso, witnesses have reported seeing your camper van at the Hayes Landing owl blind late at night on multiple occasions. What were you and your husband doing there?"

Lois looked both shocked and puzzled. "Our van? That doesn't make any sense. Fred and I always returned to the lodge early. He'd have his nightcap, take his sleeping pill, and be fast asleep in no time. Like I mentioned, I spent my evenings reading by the fire."

She furrowed her brow. "Are you sure it was our van? There are probably dozens of similar vans driving around the Adirondacks, especially with all the owl watchers in the area."

Without thinking, I blurted out the question I was dying to ask. "Did Fred know Ollie Harlow?"

Though Childress shot me a look, Lois took the question in stride. "That wildlife photographer who died? We saw him at the lodge, but no, we didn't really know him. Why do you ask?"

I tried to act nonchalant. "Just curious. I thought you might have some information that could help the police with Ollie's case. My mistake."

Childress took it from there. "Thanks for your time, Mrs. Caruso. We'll get in touch if we need more information."

As we headed for the door, Childress stopped and turned back toward Lois. "Just one last thing."

Classic cop move, saving that one last question for the end.

"You said earlier Fred took a sleeping pill last night," Childress continued. "Do you know where he kept his pill bottle?"

Lois thought about it for a moment. "It should be on his nightstand. Your team can probably find it there if they need it."

I again thanked Lois for her time and asked if there was anything else she needed. No, she said, just rest. I promised to check in on her later and we saw ourselves out.

∼

As I escorted Childress to her car, I was itching to hear her take on Lois. "What do you think? Do you believe her?"

"Yeah, I think so," she said. "I've got a good eye for spotting phonies, and that's not fake grief. She's genuinely mourning."

"What about Fred?"

"You tell me," she countered. "Do you still think he was in cahoots with Ollie in owl trafficking?"

"Well, even though Lois denies their van was at Hayes Landing, Fred could have slipped out while she was engrossed in her romance novels," I paused for a moment. "Then again, it's just as likely that it wasn't the Carusos' van there in the first place."

Childress agreed. "And let's not forget, we still have a murderer on the loose."

That caught me off guard. "I thought maybe Fred offed Ollie to keep all the trafficking profits for himself," I said.

"Not likely," she countered. "In my experience, criminals don't usually turn on each other in the middle of the crime. Remember that trap you found at Sunset Ridge? Well, it's the same type of device the trafficking ring has used in other areas, which tells me that Ollie and his partner were still actively trapping owls. Following me so far?"

I nodded, prompting her to continue.

"Running an operation like that takes a ton of effort, and

Fred would've needed Ollie's help to see it through to the end," she explained. "So, if money was the motive behind Ollie's murder, then I highly doubt the killer and Fred's accomplice are one and the same."

As the taillights of Childress' SUV faded out of view down the driveway, my head was spinning with questions.

Fred's death threw a wrench into things, but Wildcat's account of the van spotted near Ollie's vehicle at Hayes Landing made the Carusos look pretty suspicious. Lois was as delicate as a flower—she couldn't hurt a fly, let alone someone like Ollie. So, I had been convinced that Fred was both the killer and Ollie's partner in owl trafficking.

Now, I didn't know what to think. Maybe it wasn't the Carusos' van at Hayes Landing after all, and they were innocent. On the flip side, Fred might still have been mixed up in owl trafficking, and someone else could have bumped off Ollie.

But if Fred didn't do it, then who did?

CHAPTER 25

It was nearly daybreak by the time I returned to my cabin. I twisted the knob on the bathroom faucet and splashed cold water on my face to shake off the fog from what felt like the longest night ever.

Slipping into a pair of mostly clean jeans and a flannel shirt, I contemplated my next move. With Fred out of the equation, we might never know the truth about his involvement in the wildlife trafficking ring. But Childress seemed convinced that Ollie's killer and his trafficking partner were two different people anyway, and that meant the murderer was still on the loose.

Since I was hitting a dead end trying to uncover who else was involved in the owl trafficking ring, it seemed smart to switch gears and concentrate on finding Ollie's killer.

And Mason Reed was at the top of my list.

Everyone knew about the bad blood between Ollie and Mason, but did it justify murder? Possibly. The stuff I'd found online suggested that Ollie was close to exposing Mason as a fraud, though it relied on hearsay and guesswork.

I needed solid evidence before I could bring my suspicions to Childress.

That's where Sam and Wanda entered the picture. They were my aces in the hole. Hopefully, the two of them had dug up something that would confirm Mason's motive and maybe even link him to Ollie's murder. My first move, I decided, was to catch up with Sam.

I gulped down an aspirin and headed to the lodge, where I found Fuzz and Charley dozing at the reception desk. Fuzz was slouched in the office chair, his legs sprawled out on the floor in an uncomfortable-looking position. Not wanting to disturb them, I tiptoed through the lobby and into the great room.

As I neared the kitchen, the familiar sounds of ABBA filled my ears. Inside, Evie, Maddie, and Liliana were busting moves to "Dancing Queen," the melody blasting from speakers on the shelf above the toaster. Baking utensils lay scattered across the countertop as the trio repurposed spatulas and whisks into pretend microphones.

"Join us!" Maddie shouted, shoving a spoon-microphone into my hand. I didn't have time to think, so I just plunged into the performance, singing along at the top of my lungs.

After the song ended, I had to ask what was going on.

Evie grinned playfully. "I guess we were just in the mood for dance." Noticing my skeptical look, she added, "It's probably not appropriate to dance with Fred dying and all, but it's ABBA. Who can say no to that?"

"You've got a point. There's never a wrong time for ABBA, is there?"

Maddie laughed and informed me that she'd taken the day off to help at the lodge, but Liliana was quick to set the record straight. "Actually, we both took the day off so we can run the lodge, and you and Evie can take it easy."

"Take it easy? No chance," Evie shot back, her energy

palpable. "I can't just lounge around all day. I need to stay busy or I'll lose my mind."

"Well, I might just take you up on that offer," I said. "I need to stop by Sam's place before he heads to work, but it can wait until we've got the breakfast bar sorted out."

"Why the rush?" Maddie asked. "You can catch up with Sam later."

"It might sound strange, but for a minute, I suspected Fred could be involved in Ollie's murder. Now, I'm having second thoughts," I said, sharing the insights Childress and I had gathered from Lois.

"Meanwhile, I've had Sam and Wanda taking a closer look at Mason Reed," I continued. "I'm hoping to hear that they've turned up something good. So, I figured I'd pop by Sam's house for an update before he heads to the mercantile. Speaking of which, has anyone seen Mason around recently?"

"I saw him in the parking lot last night when I was coming back to the lodge from the Hop House," Maddie said. "It looked like he was gearing up for some night photography."

"He also left a message on the landline saying he's checking out later today," Evie added.

"Then I guess I better figure out what's going on with him soon," I said.

For the next hour, I helped them prepare a full spread. Evie and I baked muffins and scones, while Liliana brewed coffee and squeezed fresh orange juice Maddie chopped fruit for a yogurt and granola bar.

By the time we were done, I was pretty hungry. I grabbed a blueberry muffin and a cup of coffee on my way out.

"No more ABBA without me," I teased as I walked out the door.

"No promises!" Evie shouted back with a laugh.

I parked the Birdmobile in front of Sam's house and quickly brushed muffin crumbs off my jacket before heading to the side entrance. Peeking through the window, I could see Sam standing in front of the stove, working a spatula.

"Morning!" I said as I stepped into his sunny yellow kitchen.

"Hey there," Sam replied, leaning in for a kiss. "I was just thinking about giving you a call."

"Oh yeah?" I said, helping myself to some coffee. "Any developments?"

He nodded. "Maybe a pretty big one."

He started off by telling me how he and Wanda has snooped around the internet to dig into Mason's background. Initially, they ran across the same information I did, including those discussions about Mason's iffy photos on the photography forums.

Then, Wanda came up with the bright idea to create a fake profile. They'd used the name ShutterbugChuck and started poking around the message boards, asking questions about Mason and Ollie.

"Before we knew it, ShutterbugChuck had connected with a bunch of photographers, mostly amateurs, but there were a few pros too. And they were all willing to dish about Mason. About a third of them were dead set that he was a phony, another third swore he was the real deal, and the rest didn't really have much of an opinion either way."

"So we're back at square one," I said. "If Mason really is a phony, then Ollie was on to something, and Mason had a motive to shut him up. But if Mason's the real deal, then Ollie's accusations don't mean squat. Mason could just debunk them and write Ollie's accusations off as sour grapes. No real threat equals no real motive."

"Hold on," Sam cut in. "There's more. Someone going by the username 'MissTwist' messaged ShutterbugChuck last night. She noticed Chuck's profile said he's from Beechtree, and she claims to have solid evidence that Mason's photos are fake. Long story short, Wanda and I arranged to meet MissTwist in person this morning."

"I'll admit that sounds promising, but meeting up with someone you met online seems a bit risky, doesn't it? Should I tag along for backup?"

"No need," he replied confidently. "Wanda and I have it under control. We've arranged to meet her at her hotel in Lake Placid. It should be safe enough."

We decided to meet up again later that afternoon, once Sam and Wanda got back from meeting MissTwist. When it was time to leave, I planted a quick kiss on his cheek, reminding him to stay safe. "The last thing I need is a busted-up boyfriend."

"Would it make you feel better if I wrapped myself in bubble wrap for extra protection?" he joked.

Part of me thought that might not be a bad idea.

Climbing into the Birdmobile, I turned the key in the ignition and let the engine warm up a bit. Against all odds, Sam and Wanda might actually be onto something. If they managed to uncover solid evidence that tied Mason to Ollie's murder, or even just something that gave him a motive, it could change everything.

My phone buzzed, and I glanced at the screen. The number wasn't familiar, so I shifted the Birdmobile into drive and pulled away from the curb, navigating through the village streets.

By the time I reached Main Street, my curiosity got the best of me. I pulled over, tapped on the voicemail icon, and listened to the message.

"Hello, Ms. Palmer, Tyler Barnes from the Adirondack

Daily Herald. I heard there was another unfortunate event at Loon Lodge last night, and I'm wondering if you'd like to comment. Fair warning, I'm running another story in tomorrow's paper, but I thought you might want to set the record straight. Hope to hear from you soon."

My patience with Tyler Barnes was wearing thin. His constant jabs at the lodge were starting to grate on me, but if he thought he could tarnish the lodge's reputation again, he had another thing coming.

Game on, Tyler Barnes. Game on.

CHAPTER 26

I dragged myself through the door of my cabin. My arms felt heavy as lead, and I could barely keep my eyes open. Thirty years ago, pulling all-nighters was my thing. I could stay up studying the entire night, then breeze through the day without so much as a yawn. Now, even a few hours of missed sleep left me feeling completely drained.

With the lodge in the hands of the three dancing queens, I decided to catch some shuteye before I met up with Sam and Wanda to hear about their meeting with MissTwist.

Kicking off my boots, I sank into the couch cushions and cocooned myself in one of my mother's old quilts. The familiar trumpet of the Monk theme song filled the room as I started up an episode for background noise. My eyelids grew heavy, and I snuggled deeper into the quilt, feeling it rise and fall with each breath.

I was out cold before Monk even found his first clue.

In my dream, I found myself alone on a snow-covered tundra, the wind whipping icy flakes across my face like tiny needles. The only light came from a distant, cold star and a faint sliver of moon struggling to break through the swirling snow.

Suddenly, a silent shadow detached itself from the darkness and glided effortlessly toward me. Its ghostly white form blended seamlessly with the snow, nearly invisible except for the two piercing yellow eyes that locked onto me with unsettling intensity

I stumbled back clumsily, my foot catching on a hidden snowdrift. The impact knocked me off balance, and for a moment, everything spun, and the white landscape merged the sky. Before I could gather myself, the owl swooped down. Its massive form cast a shadow over me, blocking out the feeble moonlight.

In an instant, the scene shifted. Now I found myself in the lodge's great room. Flames crackled in the fireplace as Tyler Barnes lay bound and gagged on the rug in front of the hearth.

Dipping a feather quill in ink, I proceeded to draw a curly mustache and monocle on his face. "Not so smug now, are you Tyler?" I chuckled. In my fantasy, he whimpered through his gag, staring up at me through pleading eyes. I waved the quill menacingly and he flinched.

Payback felt surprisingly sweet.

Rubbing the sleep from my eyes, I glanced at my watch and realized I'd snoozed way longer than I'd intended. It was pushing one o'clock already. I quickly brushed my teeth to cleanse the stale sleep taste from my mouth, threw on my parka, and headed over to the lodge to check on Evie and the girls.

Liliana greeted me with a bright smile at the front desk. "Any updates?" I asked, crossing my fingers, hoping that we'd managed to avoid any new crises.

"Just the usual. I gave Fuzz and Charley the afternoon off,

Maddie's rallying the housecleaning crew, and Evie's in the kitchen."

Although I offered to take over at the front desk, Liliana wouldn't have it. She insisted she had everything under control and shooed me away.

I found Evie sitting at the kitchen table, polishing off a sandwich with a creamy, yellow filling. "There's more in the fridge if you're hungry," she offered.

"Egg salad?" I guessed, wrinkling my nose a bit.

She confirmed it with a nod. "No thanks," I replied, tossing an everything bagel into the toaster oven.

"How are you doing?" I asked, leaning against the counter while I waited for my bagel to toast.

"It's been pretty quiet around here, to be honest," she replied. "Not as many folks at breakfast anymore. And hardly any new reservations the past few days."

"Looks like things might start getting back to normal soon," I said. Before long, the timer dinged, and I retrieved my bagel from the toaster, slathering it with a schmear of cream cheese. "How's Fuzz holding up?"

Evie smiled. "He's hanging in there, just exhausted like the rest of us. I spent some time with him at the front desk earlier, and he didn't even make his usual pitch about getting married, so he must be tired."

I took a bite of my bagel, relishing the blend of seeds and cream cheese on my taste buds. "You won't believe what Sam and Wanda have gotten themselves into," I said. Between bagel bites, I recounted the story Sam had told me earlier, including the details of their planned rendezvous with Miss-Twist in Lake Placid.

"MissTwist says she has solid evidence that Mason Reed's photos are fake," I explained. "I'm heading over to Sam's place again this afternoon to see what they've uncovered. Want to tag along?"

"Absolutely," she replied instantly.

A few hours later, Evie and I were seated in Sam's living room with him and Wanda. Although Wanda could barely contain her excitement, Sam's expression was harder to read.

"Alright Sam, don't keep us in suspense any longer," I said. "What happened with MissTwist?"

"And don't spare the details, we want to hear everything," Evie added.

Sam sat up straight. "Well, we met her at the hotel restaurant, like we planned. She was really nice, super friendly," he began. "And get this, she didn't even bat an eye when we came clean about ShutterbugChuck not being real."

"ShutterbugChuck was my idea!" Wanda proudly interjected.

"Anyway," Sam continued, "right out of the gate, MissTwist told us Mason Reed is a complete fraud."

Wanda jumped in, eager to share her part. "Then, I asked her why she was so sure Mason was a phony. Honestly, I expected her to spout some wild conspiracy theory. The people you meet on these message boards can be kind of out there."

I had to hold back a laugh, imagining MissTwist probably thought the same thing about Wanda.

"But instead of a conspiracy theory," Sam went on, "MissTwist dropped a bombshell. She confessed that she was the one who faked Mason's photos for him. She offered to prove it too. Took us right up to her hotel room and showed us her whole setup."

"She had all kinds of equipment in there," Wanda added. "Computers, huge displays, stacks of hard drives. I don't know anything about editing pictures, but it looked pretty impressive to me."

I was on the edge of my seat now. "Did she actually show you how she doctored Mason's photos?"

"She sure did," Sam said. "Pulled up the originals Mason gave her, then walked us through the whole process of how she manipulated them into those award-winning shots."

He shook his head in disbelief. "It was incredible to see her take a mediocre photo of a wolf and turn it into that iconic shot with the northern lights in its eyes. She totally fabricated all the little details that made it look completely real."

According to MissTwist, Mason would secretly visit her hotel each night. She'd take the photos he'd snapped as raw material and then work her magic to radically alter them. What started as mundane and frankly subpar nature photographs would end up looking like stunning works of art.

MissTwist also let slip that Mason was clever about making sure people the right saw him taking photos both during the day and sometimes at night. That's how he kept up the facade that all of his amazing wildlife shots were legitimate.

I leaned back, completely floored. This was a game-changer. If Mason's photos really were fakes, then he had a solid motive for bumping off Ollie, to protect his secret. This was exactly the kind of proof I'd been hoping for—and then some.

"Wait a minute," Evie interrupted. "Why would this woman just tell you all of this stuff. It seems risky. She was basically an accomplice, right?"

"Well, they had a bit of a falling out," Sam continued. He explained that Mason had been paying MissTwist a good chunk of change to doctor his photos. Once Ollie was out of the picture, Mason figured he could save a few bucks. He told her that from now on, he'd only pay her a fraction of what he used to.

"As you can imagine, she didn't take too kindly to that,"

Wanda added. "I guess she thought outing his secret was the ultimate payback. And she looked pretty pleased with herself about it too."

"She wasn't very happy about that," Wanda chimed in. "Guess she thought exposing his secret was the ultimate payback."

Even though it was looking more and more like Mason was our guy, there was still one question I needed answered. "Any chance MissTwist knows where Mason was the night Ollie died?" I asked.

Wanda and Sam exchanged an uneasy glance. Eventually, Sam shared that Mason and MissTwist were more than just business partners. When Evie pressed him for more details, Sam took a deep breath and dropped the news that according to MissTwist, Mason was with her the night Ollie was killed.

"The whole night," Wanda said. "There were holed up in her room playing hide the . . ."

"I get the picture," I interrupted. "So you're telling me Mason has an alibi?"

"I'm afraid so," Sam sighed. "Although Mason is probably guilty of fraudulent photography, he wasn't behind Ollie's murder. His alibi seems solid."

I slumped back on the couch, frustrated. "I just don't get it," I muttered. "Then who killed Ollie?"

Wanda shrugged. "I've got nothing. I'm stumped."

"We must be missing something," Evie piped up. "Something we've overlooked."

I racked my brain, coming up empty every time. We'd chased down every lead, looked at every suspect, and had nothing to show for any of it.

Sam gave my shoulder a reassuring squeeze. "Don't worry, we'll figure this out. Things always have a way of working out in the end."

As Wanda headed off to get the cafe ready for the evening rush, I told Sam that dinner was on me tonight. I wanted to make something special to show my appreciation for all his hard work.

The drive back to the lodge with Evie was quiet, both of us wrestling with the reality that we were no closer to solving Ollie's murder than the day his body was discovered at the owl blind.

When I dropped Evie off at her and Fuzz's cabin, I decided to pop in to check on Lois. Something felt off the second we stepped through the door. Charley lay sprawled out in front of the fireplace, totally knocked out, and there was no sign of Fuzz or Lois.

The cabin's emptiness and Charley's vegetative state sent alarm bells ringing in my head.

Something was wrong, but I had no idea what it was.

CHAPTER 27

I stood in the middle of Fuzz's cabin, hands planted on my hips, scanning the empty living room. "Where is everybody?"

Evie emerged from the bedroom. "No sign of them back there." As she began scouring the rest of the cabin for hints about where Fuzz and Lois had gone, I peered at the back porch through the screen door. It was deserted except for Fuzz's rocking chair, swaying with the wind.

Charley gave a loud snore from his spot in front of the fireplace, his legs twitching as he dreamed. I went over to him and crouched down, gently smoothing his ears back. He appeared to be breathing normally, he was just really out of it.

Evie looked worried. "When have you known Fuzz to go anywhere without Charley?"

"Maybe he had to run out for something and decided to let Charley sleep," I said, not really buying my own explanation.

Standing up, I pulled aside the curtain and glanced out

the front window. Though I hadn't noticed it when we pulled in, Fuzz's pickup was missing from its usual spot. "Look, his truck's gone," I pointed out. "I'll bet he took Lois to grab a bite to eat."

We checked the cabin one more time. Apart from a rumpled throw blanket on the couch and a couple of dirty mugs in the sink, everything else was in order. But there was no note, and nothing to indicate where they might have gone.

I whipped out my phone and dialed Fuzz's number. It went straight to voicemail. I left a message asking him to call me back immediately. Then Evie and I decided to head to the lodge, hoping Maddie and Liliana might know where Fuzz and Lois had disappeared to.

Passing the parking lot, we noticed Lois' camper van was also missing from its usual spot. "So much for the idea that they just went out to eat," Evie said. "Why would they need both vehicles?"

As we walked toward the lodge entrance, Mason Reed suddenly burst out of the door, lugging a suitcase. When he spotted us, he hoisted his suitcase and beelined across the snow-covered lawn, bypassing the cleared path.

"He seems to be in a hurry to get out of her," I murmured.

Inside, we found Maddie and Liliana at the front desk. Liliana commented that Mason had just checked out.

"Yeah, we noticed," I responded, then quickly filled them in on Mason's photography scheme. "He likely beat it out of here when he found out we were onto him."

Then, I explained our situation and how we were trying to locate Fuzz and Lois. Their vehicles were missing, and Charley was comatose back at Fuzz's cabin. "Any idea where they could be?"

As we put the pieces together, we realized that none of us had seen Fuzz or Lois since Liliana took over Fuzz's shift at the front desk that morning. I tried to downplay our concern, but Evie was growing more anxious by the second. Honestly, so was I.

Finally, Evie had enough. "I can't just sit here," she said, heading for the door. "I'm going out to look for him."

I told her to hold on and insisted we'd search for Fuzz together. Liliana said she'd take care of Charley, and Maddie agreed to call us if Fuzz or Lois turned up at the lodge.

We began by checking Fuzz's usual haunts. The hardware store was a bust—they hadn't seen him all week. The bait shop was next, but no sign of Fuzz there either, though the owner did wonder if I'd ask Fuzz if he wanted to go ice fishing the following Wednesday.

After striking out at the bait shop, I called Wanda to see if Fuzz had turned up at the cafe. She checked with her staff, but no one had seen him for several days. When she tried to engage me in a rehash of her conversation with Mason and MissTwist, I cut her off, explaining I was in a rush.

On the off chance Sam stopped by the mercantile, Evie and I decided to check in with Sam. We found spotted him behind the counter, haggling with a customer over the price of a hooded sweatshirt. I caught his attention and motioned him over to the side.

I told him about Fuzz and Lois's disappearance, and wondered if he'd seen them. Unfortunately, he hadn't, and while he wanted to help us look, he was swamped at the mercantile. One of his employees had left early with a migraine, and he was drowning in a sea of customers looking for last-minute souvenirs before leaving town. Still, he promised to give us a shout if they showed up.

Back at the Birdmobile, I turned to Evie. "I'm running out of places to look. I think we need to consider the possibility that something is seriously wrong."

"I'm really starting to worry about him," she replied, concern etched on her face.

"I think we can rule out the idea that Fuzz and Lois went out to grab lunch or a tube of toothpaste," I said. "This has to be tied to Ollie's murder somehow. What are we missing?"

"We've ruled out Mason and the Carusos, so the only person left who's been acting weird is Twilla," she pointed out.

I shook my head. "Trust me, it's not Twilla, but something else you said has me thinking. We've been operating under the assumption that the killer is a guest at the lodge, right? What if they're not?"

Evie eyes widened, like a lightbulb had just gone off in her head. "What about Wildcat Hayes?"

I was skeptical at first, but Evie made a compelling argument. Wildcat was the sole witness who claimed to have seen the Carusos' vehicle at the owl blind, and she had no proof to back her story. It was entirely possible she had murdered Ollie and concocted the story about seeing the Carusos' van to throw us off track.

The pieces were falling in place. Even though it was Fuzz's idea to pay Wildcat a visit, she'd planted the seed in his head by approaching me at the cafe and asking me to pass along her "hello." She probably figured that once we pieced together the fact that she and Fuzz were old pals, we'd end up questioning her to determine whether she'd anything strange at the owl blind. And that was exactly what we did, giving her a perfect opportunity to cast suspicion on the Carusos.

"I can't figure out how she might have done it, but is it possible Wildcat has done something with Fuzz and Lois?" I wondered out loud.

Evie's voice shook a little. "I'm not sure, but we won't solve anything just sitting here speculating."

I shifted the Birdmobile into drive and floored the accelerator. The tires let out a loud screech as we took off, racing up Main Street towards Hayes Landing.

As we sped along, the buildings outside became a blur, and a heavy silence settled in the car, thick with our shared worries and the pressing need to uncover out the truth.

CHAPTER 28

The Birdmobile's tires skidded and slid as we tore down the icy back road to Hayes Landing. Evie sat quietly beside me, her hands gripping the Subaru's dashboard. I had no idea what awaited us at Wildcat's place, but the possibilities swirled through my head like snowflakes, each one blurring into the next.

Approaching the owl blind, I caught sight of Fuzz's truck and Lois' camper van parked side by side. I hit the brakes hard and swung into a spot next to Fuzz's truck. Evie bolted out of the vehicle before I could even shift it into park.

By the time I got out, Evie was already inspecting Fuzz's truck, her head inside the driver's side door. I hurried over to her, opening the passenger door to take a look.

Inside, we found the usual chaos of Fuzz's world—coffee cups and snack wrappers everywhere, with dog biscuits littered across the seats and floor. Fuzz's phone was on the console, which explained why he hadn't answered my calls. Despite the clutter, nothing seemed amiss, other than the fact that Fuzz's truck was here while its owner was not.

Moving on, we turned our attention to Lois' van. Unlike

Fuzz's truck, the van's cab was neat and pristine. The rear curtains were drawn, so we couldn't see much of the interior living area, and when I tried the side door, it was locked. Wherever Fuzz and Lois were, they hadn't left any clues behind in their vehicles.

I looked around, hoping to spot something that might point to where Fuzz, Lois, and maybe even Wildcat had gone. The snowy ground was a web of footprints leading in all directions, weaving paths between the parking lot and the owl blind.

One set of footprints caught my attention. Among the myriad tracks criss-crossing the area between the parking lot and the owl blind, three sets stood out. They veered off toward the edge of the airfield instead of looping back to the parking area.

"Evie, look at this," I said, pointing at the distinct set of tracks.

She joined me, zeroing in on the largest footprints. "Those have got to be Fuzz's, he's the only person I know with size thirteen boots around here," she said. "Which means the two smaller sets of prints..."

"Must be Lois's and Wildcat's," I concluded.

I dashed back to the Birdmobile to grab my hiking backpack. It was stuffed with outdoor essentials and a few emergency items like a flashlight, space blanket, flare gun, and even some old candy bars. Strapping it on my shoulders, we set off following the trail of prints..

About halfway down the airfield, the footprints abruptly turned into the woods. A wave of uneasiness washed over me as we stepped into the dim forest, the setting sun casting a pale glow through the tree branches.

What had possessed Fuzz and Lois to follow Wildcat out here? And more importantly, where was she taking them?

As we pressed further into the forest, my anxiety deepened. The tracks hugged the edge of the airfield, tucked just within the tree line, and eventually led us deep into the woods at the end of the unused runway.

Stopping to catch my breath, I asked Evie whether we were sure the prints belonged to Fuzz, Lois, and Wildcat. Her determined look was all the answer I needed. We weren't turning back now.

With daylight fading fast, we soon had to rely on the beam of my flashlight to see the trail of footprints. I was about to suggest turning back when the faint sound of voices drifted through the air.

We exchanged a look and crept slowly ahead. The voices grew louder. I switched off the flashlight and gestured for Evie to stay low. Crouching behind a large oak, I eased the backpack off my shoulders and retrieved my binoculars.

Through the lenses, I spotted three figures in a small clearing ahead, illuminated by the dim glow of a lantern. Even in the meager light, there was no mistaking Fuzz's towering presence, or Lois' petite stature. Wildcat stood opposite Lois, waving her arms in a threatening manner as she spoke.

No one looked happy to be here.

Lowering the binoculars, I handed them to Evie so she could see for herself.

"We need to get closer to hear what they're saying," she whispered. "Maybe even try to take out Wildcat."

I didn't have a better plan, so I volunteered to circle around and catch Wildcat off guard. This would allow Evie to approach from the front as a diversion.

"Not a chance," she said, her eyes burning with a tenacity I'd never seen before. "Wildcat's mine."

I opened my mouth to protest, but Evie had already slinked into the underbrush, using trees and shadows as cover. With a sigh, I headed in the opposite direction, treading lightly through the night.

Stopping to assess the situation, I concealed myself behind a large pine tree, its thick, knotted trunk wide enough to hide my generous frame. From there, I had a clear view of Wildcat from the front, with Lois and Fuzz positioned so their backs were partially turned toward me.

Wildcat was clearly agitated, her movements sharp and angry. Although I couldn't make out what she was saying, her animated gestures made it clear that she was directing her fury at Lois.

I continued moving stealthily through the trees for a better vantage point. From the side, the scene came into sharper focus. No wonder Wildcat was so upset—Lois was holding a pistol at waist height and pointing it directly at Wildcat.

Evie and I had completely misjudged the situation. Though I was still piecing together Wildcat's role, Lois was far from the delicate flower we thought she was. In fact, standing there with a gun in her hand, she looked downright scary.

Suddenly, it all made sense. How could I have been so oblivious?

Peeking out from behind a tree trunk, I saw Evie hiding in the bushes just behind Wildcat, ready to pounce. But with Wildcat blocking her view, it appeared as though Evie still thought Wildcat was the threat—she had no idea that Lois was the real danger.

I needed to intervene without drawing attention to us. Shouting was out of the question, so I decided to move closer and try to signal Evie before she made her move.

Realizing I had to act quickly, I tried to catch Evie's eye without alerting Lois. However, Evie was so focused on Wildcat that she didn't even notice me.

Without warning, Evie sprang out from her hiding spot, brandishing a large branch. She swung the branch at Wildcat's head, and Wildcat crumpled to the ground with a thud.

At that moment, Lois swiveled the barrel of the gun toward Evie, and every hair on my body stood on end. We needed help and we needed it fast. But when I took out my phone to text Childress, I found myself staring at zero bars.

Without cell reception, we were on our own—and the situation was much more dire than I'd ever thought possible.

CHAPTER 29

*E*vie bolted to Fuzz's side, paying no mind to Lois and the handgun aimed their way. From my vantage point, I could see Wildcat laid out on the ground. Fuzz and Evie looked alright for now, but I was concerned about how long they'd stay that way. I needed to come up with something fast.

Straining to hear, I caught Fuzz asking Evie what she was doing there. "Looking for you, you old coot," she retorted. "What's your excuse? What are you doing out here?"

Cautiously, I edged closer to hear more clearly. With Lois' pistol trained on them and their hands in the air, Fuzz explained to Evie that he'd dozed off at the cabin right around lunchtime. When he woke up, Lois was gone and Charley totally knocked out. Then Wildcat called and said Lois' van had returned to the owl blind. So, Fuzz zoomed over to Hayes Landing as quick as he could, leaving Charley sound asleep at the cabin.

He found Wildcat waiting for him at Lois' van. "She saw Lois head into the woods, so we followed her. Then she whipped out a gun, and before I knew it, you clobbered Wildcat over the head with a tree branch."

Evie faced Lois with a defiant look. "Okay, Lois, what's going on?"

"Not that it's any of your concern, but I'm wrapping up some unfinished business," Lois answered, adjusting her grip on the pistol. "I would have been out of here already if it weren't for Fuzz and that crazy woman on the ground."

Fuzz looked confused. "What business could you possibly have in these woods?"

I considered my options. I could bum rush Lois and hope for the best, or I could try to talk my way out of the situation. Given that our last bum rush attempt had left Wildcat unconscious, I decided to go with diplomacy.

Stepping out of the shadows, I entered the dimly lit clearing. "The business of wildlife trafficking, right Lois?"

Lois spun around, her face registering surprise. She quickly aimed the pistol at me and with a flick of her wrist, motioned for me to stand beside Fuzz and Evie.

"What would you know about that?" she snapped.

"I know Ollie was trafficking snowy owls, and I know that you and Fred were helping him."

Fuzz and Evie looked at each other, completely blindsided by my revelation. Lois, however, took the accusation in stride, unfazed.

I decided to push my luck. "Actually, I'm pretty sure you and Fred are behind Ollie's murder too."

This time I struck a nerve. Lois' eyes blazed with anger. "That's a lie!" she shouted. "I had nothing to do with Ollie's death. That was all Fred's doing."

"Can someone please explain what's going on?" Evie asked, clearly exasperated.

Lois let out a long breath, the fight draining out of her. Lowering the piston, she murmured, "It's complicated."

"Ollie and I knew each other from our college days," she continued. "We had a real connection, but life got in the way and we drifted apart. Then, out of the blue, we reconnected on Facebook a few years ago. It was like we just picked up right where we left off."

Lois stared into the darkness, deep in thought. In the lantern light, I noticed the deep line around her eyes and mouth. She looked tired and old.

"Over the years, Fred and I sometimes dabbled in wildlife trafficking to make ends meet," she confessed. "When Ollie mentioned he needed money, I brought him into the business. Then, one thing led to another and . . . well, we ended up falling in love."

Her shoulders drooped. "Ollie hated the idea of trapping and selling wildlife, but he was desperate, and the owl irruption was going to be a nice payday for him. He swore it would be the last time."

"Did Fred know about you and Ollie?" I asked.

Lois shook her head. "We were always careful. At the lodge, I'd wait until Fred took his sleeping pill, then go downstairs to read. When the coast was clear, I'd sneak out to meet Ollie."

"So, Wildcat really did see your van at the owl blind all those nights," Fuzz said.

"Yes," Lois confirmed, her voice tight. "Earlier this week. Fred started acting strange, suspicious, and I wondered if he knew about me and Ollie. Then the night Ollie died, I somehow fell asleep right after our evening tea and slept through the night. That hadn't happened for years."

She paused, her eyes shimmering with unshed tears. "Early the next morning, Fred and I went to check the owl traps at Hayes Landing. That's when I found Ollie . . ." Her voice trailed off, choked with emotion. "When I confronted

Fred, he admitted he did it. He said he knew about Ollie and me and wanted to 'set things straight.'

Lois's face twisted in anger. "The bastard even confessed to slipping sleeping pills into my tea so he could go to the owl blind and kill Ollie without me knowing."

"Hang on," Evie cut in. "What about that whole owl attack thing? Did Fred kill Ollie with those talons Twilla found?"

Lois let out a bitter laugh. "Fred made it look like an owl attack, but he wasn't very clever about it. He bashed Ollie's head in with a hiking stick and and then used some old great horned owl talons to make it look like an attack. When he got back to the lodge, he stashed the talons in Twilla's storage contain to frame her."

"I believe you when you said Fred killed Ollie," I said. And I really did. Lois' emotions were real. "But what I still don't understand is what you're doing out here now."

"After Fred murdered Ollie, he insisted we continue with the owl trapping. I went along with it, even though I was sick about Ollie. Running the operation by ourselves wasn't easy, it was a real struggle to keep up. Eventually, I hit my limit." A hint of pride flickered across her face. "So, last night I decided to dose Fred's hot toddy with enough sleeping pills to kill a rhino."

"Wait a minute," Fuzz interjected. "You didn't drug me too, did you?"

A mischievous smirk played at the corners of Lois' mouth. "I had to check the traps before I left town, and I still had Fred's pills in my purse last night. So, yes, I slipped a couple into your tea at lunch, just to put you out for a while. To be safe, I even gave one to your poodle, tucked into a piece of cheese."

Fuzz's face turned stormy. He was visibly more upset about Charley being dosed than he was about the fact that

Lois had dosed him too. It was hard to say what he might have done if Lois hadn't still been holding the pistol.

"I really didn't have a plan after checking the traps. I knew it was only a matter of time before the cops figured out I'd drugged Fred. But honestly, it didn't matter," she said. "With Ollie gone, I didn't see much left to live for anyway."

When she spoke again, her voice was thick with emotion. "Ollie was my whole world. We'd reconnected after all those years apart and it was like we were young again. I loved him so much."

The pistol slipped from Lois' fingers and clattered to the ground as she began to weep. I moved closer, quietly picking up the gun and slipping it into my coat pocket.

Fuzz and Evie finally relaxed their hands, and the three of us looked on as sobs wracked Lois' tiny frame. Watching her anguish, I almost pitied her.

Almost.

CHAPTER 30

I woke up to the sound of loud banging on my cabin door. Bleary-eyed, I rolled over and squinted at the clock. Seven-thirty. Who in their right mind would be knocking at this hour?

Last night had been another long one. After accompanying Lois and a battered Wildcat back to the owl blind and calling 911, Fuzz, Evie and I had spent hours answering questions for the police. By the time I stumbled back to my cabin, I could barely keep my eyes open.

Now someone was pounding on my door like the place was on fire. I thought about ignoring it and going back to sleep, but the knocking only grew louder.

With a groan, I dragged myself out of bed, threw on my old flannel robe and shuffled to the door. I was quite a sight —hair sticking up every which way, face creased with pillow marks. But hey, anyone rude enough to wake me at dawn deserved to see me at my worst.

I swung open the door, fully prepared to give my early morning visitor a piece of my mind. My grumpy tirade died on my lips when I saw who it was. Childress stood on my doorstep holding two steaming to-go cups of coffee.

"Rise and shine, sleepyhead."

I blinked in surprise. After the chaos of the previous night, the last person I expected to see was Childress.

"Come on in," I said, opening the door wider.

She stepped inside and I shut the door behind her. We moved to the kitchen table and I sank gratefully into a chair, wrapping my hands around the hot cup.

"What's up?" I asked after taking a long slurp of coffee. "Don't tell me there's been another murder already."

Childress grinned. "No, nothing like that. I just thought I'd swing by on my way home, give you the latest updates on the case."

SHE SET her cup on the table and continued. "Consider the coffee a thank you for being so cooperative during the investigation. I know it wasn't easy keeping quiet, but you handled it like a pro."

"No problem. Anything to help take down those traffickers." I hid a yawn behind me hand and took another sip of coffee, hoping the caffeine would work its magic. "Though I do have some explaining to do with Fuzz and Evie. They weren't very happy about being kept in the dark about the owl trafficking."

Childress gave a sympathetic nod. "Sorry about that. No way around it." She rested her hands on the table. "But here's the good news: Lois is working with us. We discovered the murder weapon in her van — the hiking stick Fred used on Ollie. We even found traces of Ollie's blood on it."

"That settles it then. Fred's the killer."

"It seems so," Childress confirmed. "Lois insists she didn't have a hand in Ollie's murder, but she's owned up to her role in the wildlife trafficking. She's even given us detailed info on where to find the rest of the traps."

"About those traps. The one Sam and I stumbled on at Sunset Ridge—did that belong to Ollie and the Carusos?"

"Actually, it did," Childress confirmed. "Lois admitted that she and Fred misled you about the lousy birdwatching up there. They just wanted to keep you away from the area so you wouldn't discover their traps."

Curious, I asked Childress about the logistics of the owl trafficking scheme. According to Lois, Ollie was in charge of setting the traps at night, after the crowds of owl watchers had gone home. Then she and Fred would get up before dawn, retrieve any captured owls, and drive them in their van to a rendezvous point near Lake Placid. There, they passed the owls to another traffickers, who sold them on the black market.

After everything that had happened, it was still hard to fathom that sweet old Fred and Lois were involved in something so diabolical.

"Unreal," I muttered. "I just can't believe . . ."

My words trailed off as Childress' phone buzzed. She glanced down at the screen and quickly typed out a reply before looking back up at me.

"Well, here's a bit of good news. Thanks to Lois, Twilla and the DEC have ID'd the other players in the trafficking ring. As we speak, uniformed officers are placing them under arrest."

A wave of relief washed over me knowing that the ring had trapped its last snowy owl, or any other species for that matter.

Childress checked her watch. "Shoot, look at the time. You need to get dressed. We've got a meeting in twenty minutes."

"A meeting?" I asked. "What kind of meeting?"

"It's a surprise," she said, a little smile on her lips. "Go get dressed."

I wasn't sure I could handle many more surprises, but I trusted Childress. A few minutes later, Childress led me across the snow-dusted grounds to the lodge. Right away I noticed the stillness that had settled over the property. Now that the owls were gone, it was feeling like a normal January at Loon Lodge again.

The great room was deserted except for a single figure sitting at a table near the fireplace. He had his back to us as we approached.

"Who's that?" I whispered to Childress.

She put a finger to her lips. "You'll see."

As we drew closer, the man turned.

"Tyler Barnes?"

Tyler wasn't strutting around like he owned the place anymore. Surprisingly enough, he actually seemed humble. He stood up and greeted me politely, his eyes downcast and voice soft.

Childress gestured for Tyler to take a seat, her tone oozing authority.

"Listen, Tyler. I want it on record that Honey and the folks here at Loon Lodge played a crucial role in an undercover wildlife trafficking investigation. You can call my office for details. Without their cooperation, we never could have apprehended the criminals responsible for trafficking countless snowy owls and other species of wildlife across the state."

As Tyler's pen flew across his notepad, she continued. "In addition, Loon Lodge was instrumental in solving two homicides that were connected to the trafficking ring. We'll be releasing more details on those soon."

Tyler could hardly contain himself as he continued scribbling down Childress's words. When she finished, he looked up at me, his expression full of contrition and humility.

"Ms. Palmer, I . . . I never should have doubted you or Loon Lodge," he stammered. "You folks are heroes in my book. Front page news!"

He promised the full story would run in tomorrow's Daily Herald as he tripped over himself trying to make amends. After profusely thanking Childress for the scoop, he gathered his things and hurried out.

"How did you manage to pull that off?"

She smiled coyly. "I called the Herald's editor-in-chief first thing this morning. He owes me a favor."

"What kind of favor?"

Childress explained that when she was in uniform, she caught him in a rather compromising position with someone other than his wife.

"Seems to be a lot of that going around lately," I said, thinking about Lois and Ollie.

"You don't know the half of it, Honey," Childress said with a knowing laugh. "There are all sorts of clandestine relationships lurking beneath the surface around here."

Finally, I asked Childress if she'd heard anything from Big Ted. She told me that she'd notified the Beechtree PD about everything, including the fake owl attack being part of Fred's half-baked plan. Big Ted hadn't said a peep about jurisdiction.

"I think he's too embarrassed about falling for Fred's ridiculous owl attack story," Childress speculated. "He's happy to let us handle it and steer clear of the whole mess."

"I guess that wraps things up then," I said.

"For now," Childress replied. "But I'm starting think you have a knack for finding trouble."

I hated to admit it, but I was starting to think so too.

CHAPTER 31

Once more, flames flickered in the great room fireplace. The familiar crackle and hiss brought a sense of comfort, stirring memories of the countless winter evenings I'd spent in this room with the people closest to my heart.

Tonight was no different. The chatter of friends created a lively hum that drifted through the room along with the savory scents of a home-cooked meal. White linen tablecloths, bone china and polished silverware added a touch of celebration to the occasion.

Maddie and Liliana stood near the fireplace, wine glasses in hand as they chatted with Twilla and Wildcat. Maddie's eyes sparkled with laughter at something Liliana said, and she nudged her playfully. And Twilla appeared more relaxed than I'd ever seen her, leaning casually against the stone mantel.

Across the room, Wanda and Annie had trapped Childress at a cafe table, probably bombarding her with questions about the murders and the trafficking ring. I couldn't help but grin as I watched her squirming uncomfortably and glance around, no doubt plotting her escape.

Meanwhile, Fuzz was at the bar talking with Sam, while Charley darted from group to group in search of a dropped cracker or piece of cheese. Despite acting a little out of it after Lois slipped him a sleeping pill, he'd bounced back to his old, lively self in no time.

Evie and I stood nearby, taking in the scene. "Are you sure you're ready for this?"

"Ready?" she asked, arching an eyebrow. "It was my idea, remember?" Her smile lit up her face, and she glowed with excitement as she fidgeted with the pearl necklace around her neck.

I clinked my wine glass with a spoon, the sound echoing lightly through the room. "Dinner's ready!" I called out.

Everyone made their way over to the banquet table and found their places. Fuzz occupied one end with Evie seated beside him. Maddie slipped in next to Evie, and Liliana, Twilla, Childress, and Wildcat took seats across from them. Meanwhile, I settled into my chair next to Sam, at the other end of the table.

When everyone was seated, I tapped my glass again to get their attention.

"I just want to thank you all for being here tonight. I know the past few weeks have been interesting, to say the least," I began, eliciting a few giggles around the table. "But we made it through, thanks in no small part to the people in this room."

Sam lifted his glass. "Hear, hear!" Murmurs of agreement followed and more glasses were raised.

"We're just glad we could help," Liliana said. "Right, Twilla?"

"You've all been incredibly kind to me, even though I've

had to keep a few things under wraps," Twilla said with a wistful smile. "Thanks for being so understanding."

"Ah, don't mention it," Fuzz reassured her. "Undercover agent or not, you're always welcome at Loon Lodge."

"I should be thanking you, Honey," Wanda chimed in. "Investigating Mason Reed was a blast!"

"Glad you enjoyed yourself, Wanda," I said, grinning. "Let's hope the next project we work together on is a bit less . . . homicidal." A chorus of laughter followed.

"Anyway, tonight's dinner is just our little way of saying thanks. But we also have some news," I announced. "Evie, the floor is yours."

Evie rose, wiping her eyes with a napkin. "It's hard to believe it's only been six months since I arrived here. It feels like I've been part of Loon Lodge my whole life." She looked around the table. "You've all welcomed me with open arms and made me feel like one of the family. Especially this old coot," she added, turning to Fuzz.

"It was your cooking that won me over," Fuzz chuckled. "A man's gotta eat."

"Enough with the jokes, I'm being serious," she said, giving his arm a playful swat. "When you disappeared a few weeks ago, I thought I'd lost you for good. That's when it hit me how much you mean to me." She took his hand. "I've never felt this way before. I'd be lost without you."

"Aw Evie, you know I feel the same way. I never thought I'd fall in love again after Honey's mom passed away, then you came along." His eyes misted over. "Couldn't imagine life without you now."

Her hands trembled as she fumbled in her pocket. Pulling out a small velvet box, she dropped to one knee.

"Fuzz Stillman, will you make me the happiest woman in Beechtree?" She opened the box to reveal a simple gold band.

He let out a belly laugh. "Took you long enough!" He took her hands in his and added, "It'd be my honor."

Evie place the ring on his finger, tears of joy streaming down her cheeks. Then, again reaching into her pocket, she removed the diamond ring Fuzz had given her earlier in the week, and he slipped it on her finger.

The room erupted in cheers and applause. Maddie and Lilliana dabbed at their eyes with napkins, while Wanda whistled and hooted.

Suddenly, Wildcat sprang up and raised her glass. "To Evie and Fuzz!"

Glasses clinked around the table as Fuzz wrapped his arm around Evie and planted a kiss on her cheek. She rested her head on his shoulder, beaming from ear to ear.

As the night wound down, I found myself relaxing by the fireplace with Fuzz and Evie, while Charley continued scouring the floor for forgotten morsels.

"Have you two lovebirds thought about when you want to tie the knot?" I asked.

"I'm ready to elope tonight if Evie's willing," Fuzz said.

She patted his knee. "Easy, big guy. I've always liked the idea of a spring wedding. Maybe we could have it here at the lodge in May before the summer crowds arrive?"

"May it is," Fuzz agreed. "I'd marry you anytime, anywhere, but a spring wedding sounds just about perfect."

As Evie and Fuzz snuggled on the sofa, it struck me that life at the lodge was changing yet again. "I'm really going to miss our breakfast bar routine now that the owl watchers have moved on, Evie," I said. "Making muffins and chatting over coffee has been kind of fun."

"Me too," Evie responded, "but I've been brainstorming some changes for the kitchen and dining area now that things have settled down."

She elaborated on her plans, suggesting that we keep the

housekeeping crew on to manage the rooms so she could focus on the kitchen and dining area. "With a little planning, I think we could even introduce dinner service a few nights a week, open to both locals and guests. We have plenty of space, and it could really transform the lodge into a hub for the community."

"I love it!" I said. Fuzz nodded along.

Despite the whirlwind of the past few weeks, I felt completely at peace. The future held endless possibilities, but for the moment, we were all content to bask in the cozy silence, with only the gentle crackle of the fire and the sight of snowflakes swirling outside the window to occupy our thoughts.

ALSO BY BELL BECK

Death at Warblers' End

A WORD ABOUT SNOWY OWLS

Soaring across the tundra, the snowy owl (Bubo scandiacus) is a majestic predator perfectly adapted to its frigid home.

These ghostly white birds primarily inhabit the treeless plains of the Arctic, where they stalk lemmings, voles, and other small mammals. Solitary hunters, snowy owls rely on their keen eyesight and hearing to locate prey beneath the snow.

Despite their formidable size, with a wingspan up to six feet, snowy owls are surprisingly light, allowing for agile maneuvering during hunts.

While populations remain healthy overall, snowy owl numbers fluctuate dramatically depending on the abundance of their main prey, lemmings.

In boom years, when lemmings are plentiful, snowy owls raise larger broods. The surplus of young owls can lead to irruptions, large-scale southward migrations in search of food and territory. Sometimes unpredictable, irruptions can bring snowy owls to unexpected locations, including the Adirondack Mountains of New York.

The Adirondacks' open fields and frozen lakes offer an

A WORD ABOUT SNOWY OWLS

ideal winter habitat for irruptive snowies. Birdwatchers eagerly await irruption events because they provide a rare chance to witness these amazing birds outside their typical range.

However, many bird species, snowy owls included, face a growing threat: wildlife trafficking. Prized for their beauty, owls and other birds are sometimes captured illegally to be sold as pets. The illegal pet trade can disrupt bird populations and deprive species of vital breeding individuals.

So, the next time you hear about a snowy owl sighting, take a moment to appreciate this magnificent visitor. But remember, owls and other forms of wildlife belong in the wild, not in a cage.

If you suspect wildlife trafficking or any other crime harming wildlife, the U.S. Fish and Wildlife Service welcomes reports from the public. You can call their wildlife tip line at (844) 397-8477 or anonymously submit a report online.

By working together, we can help ensure snowy owls and other bird species continue to thrive in their natural habitats.

ABOUT THE AUTHOR

Bellamy Beck is a mystery writer in Syracuse, NY. Bell's cozy mysteries feature feisty female sleuths, and combine twisty plots with dashes of humor and romance. Away from the keyboard, Bell enjoys birding, kayaking, and trying to keep up with the antics of an ever-so-charming standard poodle named Charlie.

A NOTE FROM BELL

Thanks so much for joining me on this Loon Lodge adventure.

If you enjoyed this book, I'd love to keep you in the loop about upcoming releases, exclusive content, and more. Just sign up for my newsletter at BellamyBeck.com/subscribe to stay connected.

Don't forget to hop on over to Facebook to join my reader community, where you can share your thoughts and theories on the latest mysteries.

For more behind-the-scenes goodies, visit my website at BellamyBeck.com.

Stay cozy, my friend!

Copyright © 2024 by Bellamy Beck

All rights reserved.

No part of this book may be reproduced in any form or by any electronic or mechanical means, including information storage and retrieval systems, without written permission from the author, except for the use of brief quotations in a book review.

ISBN: 979-8-9894947-2-9 (Ebook edition)

ISBN: 979-8-9894947-3-6 (Paperback edition)

Made in the USA
Middletown, DE
04 August 2024